In the Company of Men

"Tadjo brings the 2014–2016 Ebola crisis into sharp focus, reminding us that it is still very much a threat to the future of humanity...[She] intertwines facts, well-known songs, legends, poems, fictionalized testimonials, and documentary prose in the stirring orality of this novel to give voice to the humanitarian disaster and to interrogate Ebola's historical and biospheric currency...Realistic, painterly, and poetic, the impeccably structured polyvocal novel registers the urgency, despair, commitment, dedication, and solidarity that Ebola provokes and leaves one at times shivering." —*World Literature Today*

"Tadjo humanizes the crisis, and the most resonant scenes bear witness to the virus as it spreads 'in silence, a thick, threatening silence, auguring even more harrowing days to come.' Brief and haunting, this makes for a timely testament to the destructive powers of pandemics."
—*Publishers Weekly*

"[*In the Company of Men*] reminds us that pandemics are world phenomena, and in doing so hits its most lyrical tone. Tadjo lets the virus speak, speak to us, and answer in the face of disaster and community, in the court of the people, animals, and trees. A necessary book today."
—Patrice Nganang, author of *Mount Pleasant* and *When the Plums Are Ripe*

"I kept talking to my Kenyan father, Ngũgĩ wa Thiong'o, about *In the Company of Men* as I read it because it resonates so deeply with our own familial history. His father left a pandemic in his village in the late 1800s and was cautioned never to talk about it, so we have no history beyond my great-grandfather. Tadjo, writing so urgently and beautifully about Ebola two centuries later at a time of Covid-19, is our witness."

—Mũkoma wa Ngũgĩ, Professor of English
at Cornell University and author of
Nairobi Heat and *Black Star Nairobi*

"In an era of accelerating translational contagions, the uncannily global resonances of Véronique Tadjo's novel grow in amplitude. This is a remarkable fiction that becomes ever more topical and probing with the passing of time."

—Russell West-Pavlov,
University of Tübingen, Germany

"[A] powerful, poetic ode to life in a country of ancient customs, ravaged by death...A magnificent and essential text."

—*Madame Figaro*

IN THE COMPANY OF MEN

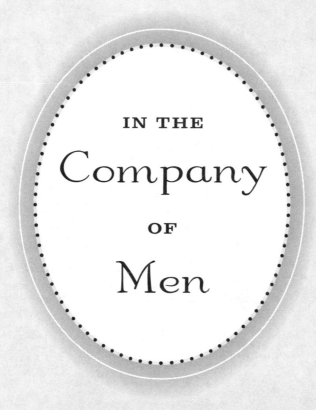

IN THE

Company

OF

Men

VÉRONIQUE TADJO

Translated by the author in collaboration with John Cullen

OTHER PRESS / NEW YORK

Originally published in French as *En compagnie des hommes* in 2017
by Don Quichotte éditions, Paris

Copyright © Véronique Tadjo, 2017
English translation copyright © Other Press, 2021

Published by arrangement with Agence littéraire Astier-Pécher

Scripture quotation on pages 65–67 taken from John 20:1, The Holy Bible,
New International Version. Copyright © 1973, 1978, 1984, 2011 by Biblica, Inc.
Used by permission. All rights reserved worldwide.

Production editor: Yvonne E. Cárdenas
Text designer: Jennifer Daddio/Bookmark Design & Media Inc.
This book was set in Bembo, Belizio and Dear Sarah
by Alpha Design & Composition of Pittsfield, NH.

3 5 7 9 10 8 6 4 2

Library of Congress Cataloging-in-Publication Data
Names: Tadjo, Véronique, 1955- author.
Title: In the company of men / Véronique Tadjo.
Other titles: En compagnie des hommes. English
Description: New York : Other Press, 2021. | "Originally published in French as
En compagnie des hommes in 2017 by Don Quichotte éditions, Paris"—Title page verso.
Identifiers: LCCN 2020031792 (print) | LCCN 2020031793 (ebook) |
ISBN 9781635420951 (paperback) | ISBN 9781635420968 (ebook)
Subjects: LCSH: Ebola virus disease—Africa—Fiction. | Virus diseases—Africa—
Fiction. | Ecology—Africa—Fiction. | LCGFT: Novels.
Classification: LCC PQ3989.2.T25 E5313 2021 (print) | LCC PQ3989.2.T25 (ebook) |
DDC 843.914—dc23
LC record available at https://lccn.loc.gov/2020031792
LC ebook record available at https://lccn.loc.gov/2020031793

FOR

THE VICTIMS IN

GUINEA,

LIBERIA

AND SIERRA LEONE

For all those whom Ebola has touched,
Whether directly or indirectly—
In other words, for all of us human beings.

*"Disasters are horrific events,
to be avoided at all costs. This is why we
need to keep our eyes focused on them,
never losing sight of them."*

JEAN-PIERRE DUPUY,
*Pour un catastrophisme éclairé:
Quand l'impossible est certain*

*"We have no choice but to march on
with a knife stuck in our backs,
since, even as we take our first breath,
we're already inscribed in
the register of the dead.
Amidst the turmoil of doubts
and aspirations,
the only gifts that count are
imagination and creativity—
they alone retain their seductive form."*

JEAN-PIERRE SIMÉON,
Lettre à la femme aimée au sujet de la mort

The
Beginning

I

Go on, get out now. Go to the capital, go to your aunt. The village is cursed. Don't ever come back here."

She stuffed some clothes into a bag and took the money he was holding out to her. She knew it was all he had left. "When the bus gets in at the main station, there will be people everywhere. But don't worry, your aunt will be there, waiting for you. Don't tell her anything. Above all, don't tell her we're dying here. That would terrify her. Don't tell her your mother and your two younger brothers are very sick. She wouldn't understand. Say as little as possible, just watch and do whatever she asks you to do. This is your chance." He gave her a quick hug and walked away without looking back.

II

Two mischievous young boys from a village on the edge of the forest went out hunting. Their village was a cluster of small houses and large circular mud huts with conical roofs and tiered layers of thatch rising all the way up to the sky. The nearby forest was an imposing presence, at once protective and nurturing, a realm inhabited by mysterious forces invisible to the naked eye. The villagers lived amid great natural beauty and utter destitution. That morning, before the sweltering, humid sun made its appearance, the entire area was bathed in mist. Armed with slings, the boys shot at everything that moved. Then they looked up and spotted a colony of sleeping bats, hanging upside down from the branches of a tall tree with rough bark. The cool,

shady foliage formed a screen against the rays of the
sun. One child took aim and hit one of the animals.
As it fell, several other bats flew off with piercing
shrieks. The boy aimed again. A muffled sound
came from the carpet of dead leaves. The other boy
took his turn, and he too hit his target. A third
bat thudded onto the ground at his feet and started
crawling feebly. The young hunters collected their
prey and proudly walked back to the village. There,
they built a log fire, skewered the bushmeat, and
seasoned it with pepper and other spices pilfered from
their mother's kitchen. Then they grilled it over the
flames, though there wasn't very much to eat: a few
chewy bones and a bit of flesh with a gamy flavor.
But it was their very own booty.

Less than a month later, the two boys
lay at death's door. Blood was flowing out of every
orifice in their bodies.

When the nurse was notified, he rushed to the
house but stopped short on the bedroom threshold
and gazed at the two boys, who were writhing on
their beds. He saw the stains of blood and mucus on
the dirt floor, smelled the stench in the air. He said to
the father: "Whatever you do, stay away from your
children. Don't touch them, don't dry their tears.
Don't take them in your arms. Keep your distance

from them. You're in serious danger. I'll call in my team." He scribbled a brief report in his notebook and hurried away to alert his superiors. But the mother didn't budge from her children's bedside. She wept as she caressed their faces and gave them sips of water to drink.

Huddled side by side in a red clay house with a tin roof, the two frail little bodies endured their suffering. Nobody knew about it. The nursing team took a long time to come. The mother couldn't just sit there and do nothing anymore. She visited the local healer to get plants for treating the sick. The man declared, "There are so many deaths, too many—this isn't normal. This sickness is not from here. Someone is out to get us. He's cast an evil spell on us that I don't know how to break. We must cleanse the village and carry out purification rites."

But in the end, he took pity on her and gave her some potions for her children. The father, waiting for the medical team to arrive, hadn't moved from the front door. He let the mother do what she wanted and watched attentively as the villagers went about their daily chores. The farmers, their hoes slung across their shoulders, walked in single file on their way to the fields. Some women with tubs of water on their heads came back from the river. Kids trotted along behind the women, clinging to their skirts, their bare feet covered with dust. Some young goats rummaged around in a pile of garbage, while chickens scraped and scratched the soil in search of earthworms. The father looked up at the yellow sun, at the rain-laden clouds, and decided that bad luck had crept into their lives.

The medical team arrived. The men got out their equipment and began to douse the ground with chlorine solution. The father stepped aside. The team ordered the mother to come out, but she refused. They erected a cordon sanitaire all around the house, and then neighbors thronged the scene, their faces still crumpled from sleep, their wrappers knotted around their chests.

The villagers watched from a distance, standing in silent groups under the trees. The father and mother looked like ghosts already, their neighbors thought. One more family gone. In the past, every new death was announced with a great deal of commotion. Cries would spread the news through the village. The women would wail and roll in the dust, tearing their hair. But now, this time, there was nothing of the sort, absolutely nothing. Everything unfolded in silence, a thick, threatening silence, auguring even more harrowing days to come. The deaths of the two boys triggered a sinister premonition that petrified the whole village.

The mother got into the ambulance with her children; it was the last time the father would see any of them alive. He barely had enough time to send his eldest daughter away. Not a single tear was shed. He was already fighting for his life.

The Whispering Tree

III

We, the trees. Our roots run all the way down
to the heart of the earth, and we can feel the
beat of her pulse. We inhale her breath. We taste her
flesh. We live and die in the exact same spot, never
moving from the land we occupy. Both prisoners and
conquerors of time, we stand riveted to the ground
yet soaring upward, reaching for the clouds. We adapt
to all weathers, rain or shine, hurricanes or the dry
harmattan winds. Our crowns merge with the sky's
cotton-wool dreams. We are the link between Man
and his past, his present, and his unpredictable future.

We exhale the fresh breath of morning. Our sap
is vital force, our souls hundreds of years old. We
see everything. We feel everything. Our memory is
intact. Our consciousness dwells beyond space and

time. We have listened to stories both happy and heartrending, and we shall witness new life cycles in the future, for such is the passage of time.

We were here to last. We were here to spread our shade over the remotest lands. We were here so that our foliage would murmur the secrets of the four corners of the world. But human beings have destroyed our hopes. No matter where in the world they are, they wage war on the forest. Our trunks crash to the ground with a sound like thunder. Our naked roots mourn the end of our dreams. You cannot destroy the forest without spilling blood. Humans today think they can do whatever they like. They fancy themselves as masters, as architects of nature. They think they alone are the legitimate inhabitants of the planet, whereas millions of other species have populated it since time immemorial. Blind to the suffering they cause, they are mute when faced with their own indifference. Their voracity is boundless; it seems impossible to stop them. The more they have—and they already have everything—the more they devour. And when they are finally sated, they turn to other cravings: commodities, money, flashy trifles. They waste what they have and grab one another's natural resources. They dig deep into the belly of the earth. They dive into the seas. They'll go on until there is nothing left.

Ah, if only they could feel the weight of our suffering! Our energy is running out, our strength is gone. We, the trees, give shelter to a world of creatures, a world that is itself its own rainbow: birds and insects, climbing plants, flowers, mosses, and lichens come and seek refuge in our arms or along the length of our bark, be it smooth or rough. Other living beings may rest in our branches, or hunt there, or eat there: shoots and buds, fruits and tender leaves. With our breath, we replenish the air and slake its thirst for oxygen.

I am Baobab, the first tree, the everlasting tree, the totem tree. My crown touches the heavens and offers the world below refreshing shade. I yearn toward soft, life-sustaining light, that it may brighten humanity, illuminate darkness, and soothe fear.

Alas, all too many of us have gone, only to be replaced by flimsy shrubs, barely able to take root. When we go, flowers and other plants lose their finery. Animals no longer find refuge. Men turn our branches into firewood and bleed our trunks. To reach and exploit an area where trees of great age and wisdom stand, men ruthlessly cut down everything in their path. They see in us nothing but marketable goods. Just look at our soil, how parched it is, how devoid of nutrients! Rich, fragrant humus turns to dust, leaving nothing but hard, impenetrable rock. I have watched animals starve to death, depriving us of their friendship.

And yet, did you know that no other terrain shelters as many living creatures as the forest does? Were you aware of that? Our roots go searching for water. Our leaves call the rain. Not torrential rain that brings devastation, but gentle, caressing showers that enfold plants and animals in their embrace. Without us, avalanches, landslides, and mudflows wreak havoc, laying waste to vast swaths of land.

We, the trees, like to believe ourselves the custodians of rivers, streams, and seas. Even far inland from a river's mouth, we make its bed and prevent it from overflowing its banks and drowning people. We dare to think we can talk to the water—the flowing water, the dancing water, the singing water. If only Man were more clear-sighted! If only he could foresee his own decline, the depletion, the degradation. Maybe he would finally understand that he depends on us, and that in this century beset by so many disasters, hundreds of forest-dwelling communities have disappeared, along with their languages, their knowledge, and their beautiful traditions. If only Man could realize how misguided he is, he would surely end the violence and lay down his axes and machetes. He would silence his chainsaws, stop his bulldozers, and lock away his heavy trucks, those gigantic iron monsters that haul timber and death. None of that brings him anything good or makes him happy.

Men fight over our bodies. Men oppose those among them who want to keep living near us, with us.

We cannot go higher than the sky, since it is not possible for us to live up there. Should we go too far underground, we would hit molten magma, the core of the earth, where our survival would be just as impossible. If the temperature of the air we breathe gets too hot too fast, we all die, every single one of us. The places where we can thrive are limited. The icy North Pole is not for us, nor are the dunes of the desert. For us, life in all its richness and beauty is found only in the forest. We must hold on to what remains of the planet, so that we can keep living on land hospitable to us.

I am Baobab. The first tree, the everlasting tree, the totem tree. My crown touches the heavens and offers the world below refreshing shade. I yearn toward soft, life-sustaining light, that it may brighten humanity, illuminate darkness, and soothe fear.

Now I am old. The natural death of trees is a renewal. One day, I witnessed the noble death of a thousand-year-old tree. The entire forest went down on its knees, time stood still, and lightning fell from the sky.

I'm ready. When my hour comes, I will stretch out on the ground, offering my trunk to the gnawing insects and the lichens that feed on my flesh. I'm ready. Death does not frighten me, it is bound up with life.

But when men murder us, they must know that they are breaking the chains of existence. Animals can no longer find food. Bats can no longer find food, can no longer find the wild fruit they like so much. Then they migrate to the villages, where there are mango, guava, papaya, and avocado trees, with their soft, sweet fruits. The bats seek the company of Men.

I know that not all humans are alike. Not all of them go looking for rare, exotic species of timber to sell to unscrupulous merchants at exorbitant rates, nor do they all set fire to the bush to make ends meet. Only some of them run industrial-scale palm oil, rubber, cocoa, coffee, and eucalyptus plantations for financial gain; only a few buy up entire harvests, loading them onto enormous container barges that sail across the seas and unload their cargoes somewhere in the West after the London, Paris, and New York stock exchanges have decided on the world market prices.

No, there are also the poor, the refugees, the shoeless, who crowd into camps to flee a fratricidal war or escape a drought and the famine that follows

it. They go into the forest and clear it to plant
cassava, yams, and maize. They hunt game, the
large cane rat, and—if they can catch it—the striped
ground squirrel, as well as the shy, dainty antelopes
or the laughing monkeys that colonize the same
trees as the bats. When such animals are trapped by
members of the clan, they can stave off hunger for
a while. But then disaster strikes. They start dying
from a mysterious disease, all alone in the forest,
with no one to help them. Sometimes, the authorities
of the country learn of the outbreak and decree a
quarantine. Those who are meant to die, die, and
those meant to live, live. The city-dwellers in the
capital know nothing about this. The towns know
nothing about it. Nobody speaks of it, because it
simply does not matter. Because it is far away. The
victims are the left-behind, the forgotten ones.

   Things were not always like this. There was a
time when men used to talk to us, the trees. We
shared the same gods, the same spirits. If one of us
had to be cut down, our pardon would be begged
first. Libations would be poured on the ground,
accompanied by a whispered prayer: "Beautiful tree,
soul of our life, cool shade of our dreams, root of
our future, friend in all seasons, we implore your
forgiveness. From the bottom of our hearts, we give
thanks for your generosity. Your presence in our lives
will forever be remembered."

———

Those were the old days, in times long past, when the ancestors who founded the village would plant me right in the center of their lives. As the centuries went by, I grew into a symbol for the close link between Nature and Man. I was the Tree of Wisdom, the one to which people would turn when they wished to find an answer to the troubles of human existence. Birds perched on my branches, conversing freely. During celebrations, balafons and koras would beat the rhythm of our masked dances. The dancers' feet shook the ground, while their heads marked the passing of time, the perpetual flow of death and rebirth, death and rebirth. I used to laugh with them then. When sorrow descended upon the village, I used to weep with them. And when a revered old man departed for the realm of his ancestors, I offered the hollow of my colossal trunk to entomb him for all eternity.

Everything is different today. Nobody wants to speak of death. People say about their dead, "They are no longer here," or "They have passed away," but no one thinks of asking where they may have gone. To the graveyard? To heaven? Underground? They prefer to deny death, because they no longer have the time to think about it. Death is a failing because it disrupts their frenetic lives. It never used to be like that in my village, where death was always welcomed. Everyone accepted it, in the same way they knew that the earth must rest before it can bring forth a new harvest. To leave a deceased person alone, all by himself, was unthinkable. To keep him company was a sacred duty, and an opportunity for the villagers to come together to eat and drink, sing, weep, and dance around him. They would talk to him, reassuring him about the grave that awaited him. The words they would murmur to him came straight from the heart. They would ask the deceased to counsel them one last time. They would touch him, adjusting his ceremonial garments so that he would always look beautiful. They would celebrate his passage on earth. Death was a part of daily life; everyone addressed it in informal terms. It was familiar to them.

For as long as life was in full swing, I was their confidant. I was the one they would talk to about their joys and sorrows. About the difficulties of life. They would lay offerings at my feet and hold gatherings under my lush foliage. I was the Palaver Tree. Long, complex discussions, strictly adhering to rules of precedence and procedure, would take place around me. Someone would ask for permission to speak, stand up, and express his opinion. When he sat down again, another would get up and continue his train of thought. In this way, important decisions were taken collectively. If a conflict was brewing, any attempts to settle it took place in my presence, including the chiefs' consultations among themselves. My cool shade was the only place where lengthy deliberations could be brought to a successful conclusion; I would encourage calm. The villagers took time to listen to one another, trying to resolve the quarrels that threatened to divide them. Quite often, having considered a problem, they would decide to forgo punishment and seek instead to repair bonds that had been abruptly broken. Life decisions were taken in the cocoon of my embrace, where all topics were discussed: marriages, births, funerals, good harvests and bad, droughts, the laudable or reprehensible conduct of a young man or a young girl, divine protection, protection against sorcery, and alliances with neighboring villages. Everything revolved around my goodwill.

A great sorcerer often came and asked my advice before creating his powerful gris-gris. All the villagers would wear the amulets, around their necks, around their waists or chests, on their wrists or on their ankles. Babies were decked out with them to avert bad luck. Young girls sought them out, for they brought love and fertility. Hunters acquired them as safeguards against the dangers of the forest. "Beyond the visible world, there is a hidden, subterranean parallel universe where our life force takes the form of scattered energies," the wizard declared. He alone knew how to control those energies and ensure that they would be beneficial for the village.

But if circumstances demanded it, he also had the power to invoke the destructive forces of nature, which made life difficult and unpredictable.

That is what life was like with the people of my village. I listened to them, they listened to the rustling of my leaves. Each in his place but all together...

I am Baobab, who keeps the memory of centuries gone by, whether bruised or blessed by the gods.

I have loved human beings, and I love them still. But, with the passing of time, I have lost my illusions. My leaves are tarnished, my bark has lost its shine. When gold was discovered in our region, my village changed from one day to the next. It became warped, disfigured, because raw gold was up for grabs. Everything was ransacked so people could get their hands on the wretched metal as fast as possible. All they could think of was splashing, milling about in the river to churn up gold deposits that would make them rich overnight. At the time, one ounce of gold was worth almost two thousand dollars. Impossible to resist! To excavate large basins in which to sift through the pebbles, they set to work cutting down every single tree in sight. Now there was mud everywhere, nothing but mud; and in their minds, madness. The women even stopped making pottery and joined in, recruiting their own children to help. On their delicate little heads they were carrying buckets full of soil. The mercury discharged into the rivers to make gold particles easier to spot killed the fish, the small shellfish, the plankton and dark-green algae. So the water became acid. Toxic. Life became poisonous. Prostitution. Bars. Arms trafficking. Drugs.

The villagers turned into driver ants, formidable predators determined to annihilate everything in their path. The past had to be wiped out as well. From one day to the next, they abandoned their fields, their legends, their customs, their beliefs. The trees that crashed to the ground took climbing animals and crawling animals with them. I was deeply saddened by this, for I knew that our equilibrium had been lost, and that many animals were being forced to flee deep into the forest for safety. It was incomprehensible to me how things could have deteriorated so much so rapidly, so abruptly. I would have liked to put a stop to all this lunacy, but I was powerless. After generations of

mutual respect, the village had turned its back on me
for good.

It didn't take long before people started to fall ill.
At first they thought it was malaria. They complained
of fevers, shivering, stomach pains. They suffered
from body aches and extreme fatigue. So they went
in search of neem leaves, leaves from the Tree of
a Thousand Virtues, the generous tree that cures
malaria and repels mosquitoes. A proud and resilient
tree that doesn't ask for much, a tree that adapts to
even the poorest kind of soil, sandy or full of rocks
or almost completely barren. But then the people
remembered how, in their mad rage, they had cut
down hundreds of neem trees. So they had no choice
but to forge a path leading them ever deeper into the
forest. Weak and exhausted, they marched on, until
finally they found the beneficent tree. They stripped
off most of its leaves and fruit, packed them into
bags, and carried them home. As soon as they got
back, the women prepared herbal infusions that the
patients were given to drink several times a day. They
crushed the neem seeds to extract the oil, which
they rubbed on the patients' skin. A handful of the
sick recovered their health within a few days. But for
the others, the majority, the fever never came down.
Their strength was gone. They started spitting blood,
then vomiting blood, then excreting blood; blood
broke through all the barriers of their flesh.

Until the very last moment, some miners refused to let go of their coveted gold nuggets, clutching them in the palms of their hands. The worksite became a battlefield, a scene of sheer devastation. The gold had sown death and disaster. I watched helplessly as the disease spread like wildfire. Nothing, it seemed, would be able to stop it.

Where are true human riches to be found? In the riches of the heart, or in the riches of wealth? My village was rich, its riches were beautiful. But when the villagers wished to possess wealth, the village disappeared.

For a long time, I was a tree in despair. I missed the children's tinkling laughter, the rough hands of the old men stroking my trunk, the beauty of the women who used to fall asleep in my shade, the men whose bodies were sculpted by labor on the land. I wanted to become a tree without roots so that I could leave this arid place and migrate to happier surroundings. My life had become useless, trickling away slowly, reduced to nothing but memories.

What was destined to happen happened against my will and out of my reach.

All of a sudden, an Ebola epidemic broke out and spread through the region, becoming the most devastating outbreak ever recorded in the history of the virus. And for the first time ever, the virus even traveled all the way to the capital.

It takes between five and twenty-one days for the fever to appear in its acute and life-threatening form. First there are stabbing pains in the temples, intensely aching muscles, and a blinding headache, followed by vomiting and diarrhea, skin eruptions, a sore throat that burns like fire. In the end, the last spark of life is snuffed out as the patient gradually bleeds to death.

Simply touching another person is enough for someone to become infected. This plague is worse than war. A mother, a father, a son can become a mortal enemy. Pity is a death sentence.

I saw the devastation the epidemic wreaked upon this country, while the rest of the world did its best to stay away. Africa became the cradle of untold suffering, the place where the future of all mankind was at stake. Should the virus jump on a bus, a train, an airplane, it threatened human extinction. It could cross borders, travel on boats. It might hide in the tears of a child, in a lover's kiss, or in a mother's embrace. It reduced human beings to nothing but flesh and viscosity. The very pavement was strewn with anonymous, ravaged corpses, the bodies of men and women who simply collapsed, as though violently struck down, on one of the capital's crowded streets. How can one ever forget that raging fury, spreading at unimaginable speed and wiping out everything in its path?

But I saw courage too. There were men, women, and young people caught up in this human tragedy, determined to fight for their own survival and that of others. I myself saw people who did not think twice about offering help. I saw people arriving from all over the world, volunteers working for free to combat the disease.

In spite of the chaos, dawn continued to break, and sunset still heralded the onset of night. I saw the morning come, quivering with impatience. Once bitterness and sorrow had passed, kindness returned. Gradually, I started listening again to what humans had to say. I listened to all of them. My branches spread out and took on tremendous magnitude.

Nothing that makes human beings what they are escaped me. I want to tell their stories, to lend a voice to all those who managed to rise above fear: ordinary men and women doing extraordinary things. No matter where they are, I want to honor their bravery. The life of humans is a story we haven't yet finished telling, a story of shipwrecked sailors washed up on an island in the middle of a sea.

I am Baobab, the first tree, the everlasting tree, the totem tree. My roots reach deep into the belly of the earth. My crown pierces the sky. I seek the light that brightens the universe, illuminates darkness, and soothes hearts.

Fight
with All
Your Might,
Fight Some
More

IV

The earth is sometimes farther from Man than the moon.
A doctor in a spacesuit discovers a new universe.

The first time I entered the vestibule of the high risk area, a patient appeared out of the corridor and collapsed right in front of me. He was dripping with blood and other bodily secretions. There must have been millions of Ebola particles all over him. Inside my bulky suit, my heart was beating like a drum. The patient had to be taken back to his bed, so a male nurse and I picked him up by his arms. He was in a state of extreme agitation, shaking uncontrollably. His eyes expressed unfathomable fear. We had to sedate him. His struggling gradually stopped, and only then were we able to leave him and tend to the other patients.

At night, I have nightmares. I dream I'm still among the sick. The tent's a furnace. It's the middle of the day, the sun's beating down on the canvas. I gasp for breath, my head buzzes, I don't have my protective suit on—I'm naked, in fact, and the virus has infected me. My gums are bleeding, my soul leaving my body. I can feel it slipping away through my navel... I wake up with a start.

My room, bathed in twilight. I can make out the outline of the window against the wall and hear the whirring of the fan. The stirred air is hot; sweat drenches me. My eyelids close heavily.

But now it's morning, peeking through the curtains. Another day has begun. I get up, head to the bathroom, splash cool water on my face for a long time, and look at myself in the mirror. I'm alive. It was nothing—just a bad dream. I must ignore it, I must return to the sick. That's where I need to be, in that makeshift health center; there's no more desperate struggle taking place anywhere on earth.

Early in the morning, I pass through the entrance reserved for the staff. Most of the others arrive by minibus. They have to get up at the crack of dawn and leave the house while their children are still asleep. My colleagues include the nurses, who are so dedicated, and the psychologists, whose task is not an easy one, and the members of the various teams responsible for water, sanitation, and the burial of the dead. The cooks arrive as well, and the laundry workers, whose jobs are menial but essential. And finally, the administrators and the logisticians, in a hurry to get to their offices at the other end of the center. The volunteers, both local and foreign, feel united in their collective desire to eradicate Ebola. Then there are also the other doctors, of course, my closest colleagues.

I go inside the tent to attend the morning meeting with the staff members who were on duty during the night. The team leader delivers his report, which includes the number of deaths as well as the number of new admissions. The influx is growing all the time. The head of the ambulance drivers explains that several patients are waiting to be admitted to the center, although there are no available beds. The testing of suspected cases needs to be sped up. The nurse points out that patients who test negative are nevertheless kept at the center so they can get treated for other problems. Would it not be better to transfer them to the Main Hospital? Someone interjects that the Main Hospital has been closed since six members of their medical staff succumbed to the virus.

Next on the agenda are the tasks for the day: a female patient is refusing to eat and take her malaria medication. Only three days ago, she lost both her husband and her baby. It's a case that needs to be closely monitored. A young man who was still very communicative on admission started going rapidly downhill and is now completely unresponsive. Several patients are in an advanced stage of the illness and require urgent rehydration. A little girl's arm has swelled up enormously, most probably due to septicemia. She has received a dose of antibiotics. One of the doctors says that special attention must be paid when giving injections, since the thickness of the gloves makes these procedures risky for both patients and staff. One of the nurses reports that a patient has vomited in the courtyard. A knife has been found under his pillow. He says he'd rather kill himself than succumb to Ebola. The team leader wants to know how this knife could possibly have stayed hidden. The nurse doesn't know. The occupant of bed number six will be allowed to go home. Five patients seem to be getting better.

I go to the changing room, where I'm helped with getting dressed. I pull on my plastic suit. The strong synthetic fabric is thick, waterproof, and sealed at the wrists and ankles. Once my body is safely wrapped, I am given a transparent plastic apron as an additional protective layer. I pull on two pairs of gloves, slide my feet into rubber slippers, heavy but comfortable, and easy to put on and take off. In front of the mirror, I check that my face mask is properly in place and my goggles fit tightly. I'm ready. Patients who are already seriously ill are brought in on stretchers. The others walk, with difficulty. Their faces are like death masks already. Their eyes bulge, their bodies are emaciated.

Bending over a patient, I'm trying to find a vein. Then the needle prick, and I can insert the catheter, gently, very gently, for the skin is dry and brittle, and the pulse practically nonexistent. I'm focused, working with precision. The gloves are definitely a hindrance; one second's distraction, and the needle may pierce my flesh. Inside my suit, sweat pours from me. I can't talk, my voice is stifled. I gesticulate to the nurse to let her know what to bring me, pointing to the instruments with my fingers. My visor is blurred from condensation. Forty minutes like this, that's the maximum. Any longer, and you may faint, you may simply collapse. Forty minutes of inhaling my own breath. Sweat trickles down my arms, my torso and legs. It's boiling hot under the torrid metal roof. The rainy season should have started by now, the rays of the sun seem to be getting more and more intense. I look up, thinking of my wife and children. When will I see them again? Why expose myself to such dangers? Ebola pushes us to our very limits, presses our backs against the wall. I refuse to let the virus win the day. I can't let the disease take control, spread, and threaten my family. We must fight it. That's the price we have to pay as long as we share the same planet.

The task before us is immense—I'm aware of that. All we can do for our patients is to try to keep them going. There are no effective medicines against the virus. So the main thing is to rehydrate the patients. We give them lots of liquids, as often as possible. They also receive nutrition by mouth, but if that doesn't work, they're fed intravenously. Then they get tablets to bring down their temperature, and they're constantly monitored for any signs of gastrointestinal problems. We also give them painkillers and try to reduce their anxiety. In their weakened state, such patients easily succumb to secondary illnesses: bacterial infections, malaria, typhoid, tuberculosis. This means we're obliged to go on treating them, even if they're already at death's door. We have to do our utmost at all times. Any personal attachment is out of the question, for that would mean making myself so susceptible to my patients' suffering that I wouldn't be able to care for them anymore. All I can really do is carry on with my work, hoping that this horror will soon be over, hoping that the day will come when I can go home to forget and start my life again.

But all this is incomparably harder when the patient is a child. I remember the baby who came in one afternoon. Her mother was holding her in her arms, tightly wrapped in a blue blanket. Nothing but the tiny face was visible: closed eyelids, a fine layer of soft hair covering the forehead, the lips slightly parted, the skin as flimsy as tissue paper. The woman had to be supported by two male nurses in protective clothing. Since we were obliged to separate the baby girl from her mother, a confirmed case, we took turns feeding the infant with a syringe. Her minuscule body was fighting, resisting. At first, she was digesting the food we gave her and seemed to be gaining strength. But after a few days, she started whimpering. She didn't sleep that night, and the following morning, the milk wouldn't go down, she couldn't swallow anymore. She vomited. Not long afterward, she took a deep breath, and then she died.

Was there something we could have done to save her?

That's the question I've asked myself so often, the question that still obsesses me. The mortality rate among children is devastating, and we have no separate room for pediatric cases. They are just as contagious as adults, and the same rules apply. Yes, by the time they're dying, they're no longer children.

Was there something we could have done to save her?

The Ebola center was put up in haste to enable us to deal with the outbreak quickly. Huge trucks arrived, piled high with wooden planks, metal sheets, and plastic tarpaulins. Then technicians set to work. They built the center—a cluster of prefabricated rooms and tents—and within a few weeks, everything was ready and working. Two generators that operate nonstop provide electricity. The noise they make is an integral part of our working day. The camp is subdivided into two different zones: one zone for suspected cases only, and the other for confirmed cases. One side of the center is reserved for medical staff rooms and offices, unauthorized entry prohibited. In the absence of security guards, an orange plastic ribbon forms a barrier around the center. The entire area is so well lit, one might say it was a prison. The patients inside feel like convicts. The ground all around the place has been bulldozed to create a perimeter that no one approaches without trepidation. Triage takes place under the big tent. Two possible directions: suspected cases and confirmed cases. People waiting for their test results have to stay in the transit zone. They pray, weep, make promises to their god, and remember the important events in their lives.

The test results take at least four hours to come in. Four hours, followed by a return to normal life or isolation in the treatment zone, which is shut off from the outside world. Formerly, getting the results took four to five days. A new mobile laboratory provided by the U.S. Army has shortened the wait.

What are we doing here on earth? Why have we been put here if our existence is nothing but suffering? Some lives seem as worthless and irrelevant as the bruised fruit left over at the end of a market day. Left to rot in wooden crates, or just thrown away, it's fruit nobody wanted, and yet, only a few hours before, it was adorning the stalls.

I'm a trespasser in the kingdom of Death. This is his private domain, his empire, where he rules with absolute power. I feel like an astronaut floating in space, a thousand miles from earth. The slightest tear in his spacesuit and he's lost. The slightest tear in mine, and, just like him, I'm lost too.

Only a few of these patients are going to make it. The rest are never going to leave their beds or the treatment tent.

Who will survive? Although they all receive the same level of care, within the span of two weeks, one patient is about to pass away, while another's getting ready to go home. Another will feel better, get stronger, start to smile again, but then, suddenly, he'll give up and die. It's impossible to know. Despite our efforts, all too often, the virus wins.

In reality, the final outcome isn't up to us. How hard the sick are able to fight against Ebola depends on the natural defenses they have at their disposal, that is, it depends on their immune system, or on the virulence of the virus infecting their organism. Were the survivors in better health than the rest before they became infected? This is something of a mystery. And suppose they recovered simply because their survival instinct was stronger than the disease? The will to survive defeats the virus, it concedes, and they have the freedom to go on living a little longer. None of us knows what we have in our bellies. I myself, though I'm a doctor, have no idea how my body would react if I came down with Ebola. Chances are, I wouldn't fare any better than my patients. A woman can survive, an old man can survive, a teenager can survive. And what about me? The virus respects nobody, makes no exceptions. Incapable of rational thought, it's the kind of enemy that instinctively wants to crush its opponent. The human race itself wouldn't be enough for it.

Even in death, Ebola doesn't want to let go. Like bombs, its corpses sow destruction.

At the start of the epidemic, there was the danger that panic might spread. The army had not yet been mobilized. Soldiers were not yet ready to fire on the sick if they tried to escape. But how do you get used to the idea that your body will end up in a plastic bag, doused with disinfectant and interred in a communal grave by men in masks? Buried without any sort of ancestral ritual to prepare the deceased for entry into the next world, and without any kind of funeral to honor their memory. No time for contemplation or human affection. Some people went home in spite of their diagnosis. They "absconded," with all the consequences doing so entailed: bringing the virus back to their family, to their village, to their town.

My shift over, I return to the changing room. This time, I get help with the long, complicated process of taking off my protective suit. First, to ensure my bootsoles are free of debris or contaminated fluids, I have to step into a container filled with chlorine solution. Then I'm doused with a disinfectant. I extend my arms so that the solution can reach every part of me. Any physical contact is to be avoided. Next, I take a chlorinated shower. All the clothing I've worn must also be washed in chlorinated water and then dried in the sun. What can't be disinfected gets burned.

When a patient is allowed to go home, it makes me happy. He or she receives new clothes, since everything worn on arrival at the center has been incinerated. The patient is also given some food, vitamins, a small amount of money, and a certificate of good health, which should help with restarting a normal life. When I see a smile on a patient's face, I tell myself that I've done my duty. The things I go through in the Ebola center are extremely distressing, but I've never known anything more gratifying than alleviating human suffering.

My thoughts are with my children and what we'll do when we're together again. I'm going to buy them bicycles, one red, one blue. I'm going to teach them bicycle racing. They'll love that; it will make them happy. All I really want is to spend time with them. To stay home, play in the garden, watch television. I miss their mother. To me, she's the most beautiful woman in the world.

V

The nurse's courage is a jewel she wears
on her chest with benevolence and pride.

I care for my patients with compassion, trying
to put myself in their place, to understand what
they suffer. There's no difference between them
and me, except for the circumstances that separate
us. I'm on the other side of the barrier. But they've
done nothing to deserve what's happening to them.
We waste so much time. Our lives are frittered away
with trivialities. And now that our normal, everyday
routine is in turmoil, we should all go back to the
beginning and start again. Looking to the past for
answers is no longer an option.

It's the women who are the worst affected by the
epidemic. Maybe because it usually falls on them to
care for the sick. Maybe because they're the last to
leave home and seek treatment. And maybe because,

until the very end, they try to keep things going, they try to make things right.

When the first infected patients started arriving at the government hospitals before the outbreak was officially declared, we members of the medical staff, out of ignorance, treated them with our bare hands. Our white cotton lab coats were our only protection. It was only afterward that we were informed. Many of us took the infection home and didn't survive. I was terrified. Now that the Ebola virus has been identified, I know how careful we must be: following the hygiene rules to the letter is not negotiable, underestimating the danger can be deadly, and staying alert at all times is imperative.

I saw a very close colleague of mine become contaminated right in front of my eyes. A child arrived in a very bad state. The boy was bleeding from every orifice, he had diarrhea, and his chest was racked by spasms of deep, painful hiccups. My colleague cleaned him up and bent over him, trying to make him drink. Suddenly, he vomited all over her shoulder. Her white coat was soaked and stuck to her skin. That's how she caught Ebola. A few weeks later, she died.

When people on the outside learned you were working with Ebola patients, they didn't want to come near you anymore. You lost all your friends. When you went home, you were alone with your family. My daughter had problems at school; no one wanted to play with her during recess. Her fellow students had heard the rumors circulating in the neighborhood: the medical staff was behind all these deaths; the President of the Republic had supposedly paid them large sums of money to reduce the local population and thus get rid of the poor. Ebola, they said, didn't exist.

Despite all this, we continued fighting the disease. Watching my colleagues die, abandoned by the authorities and without any form of qualified help, was terribly hard.

In the morning, before going to see the patients, we pray. We get together and we pray. We close our eyes, stretch out our arms toward heaven, and sing hymns. We beseech God to have pity on us. Lord, give us the wisdom to know what we should do. Give us the will and the ability to accomplish it. Give us the courage to go on.

The patients are in pain, they need care and reassurance. If they believe in God, we tell them to keep their faith, but above all else, we urge them to continue eating and drinking, even when their strength is gone. We rub their backs, we hold their hands. We talk to them in their mother tongue, in words familiar to them. I would like to take off my mask to let them see who I am, to let them look into my eyes and know that I share their suffering. But that simply isn't possible.

Where should we focus our efforts amid this uninterrupted stream of patients? Will the decisions we make in the heat of the moment determine whether they're going to live or die? There's no one to tell us.

Even inside the hospital, the sick occasionally express doubts about us. They think we want to poison them with the needles we stick into their arms, or with the concoctions we make them drink. If not, why aren't they getting better? Why else would there be so many deaths among them? So they want me to take a sip of the liquid I'm holding out to them. Why not try a little bit yourself, they say, if it's really that beneficial? And then they also ask why they're not allowed to have masks and protective suits, whereas all those who come near them are wearing them. I suppose they have a point. How can we earn their trust when our equipment alienates us from them? The distance between us is the distance between life from death. To tell them otherwise would be lying.

Our hospitals have always been run on a shoestring budget. Getting by without the essentials, making do without even the minimum, is common. Poorly managed budgets, insufficient budgets, deplorable working conditions, underpaid staff: we're used to all that. Our long working hours are spent in buildings with peeling paint, where the mattresses on the iron bedsteads are filthy and all the furnishings either damaged or broken. Out-of-order machinery is just left in a storeroom. The place reeks of open wounds. We're used to all that. But this time, things are worse than ever; the lack of supplies has taken on gigantic proportions.

One day, I heard a young guy plucking the strings of his guitar and singing in a bleak, cynical voice:

Come along with me!
Let's go to the University Hospital in the capital,
The global disease market.
Let's go buy some cholera
From soiled, overflowing toilets!
Let's go buy some malaria
From the stagnant puddles in the courtyard!
Let's go buy some AIDS
From all that medical waste!
Let's go buy some madness
From sacks of corruption and arrogance!
Come along with me!
Let's go to the University Hospital in the capital,
The arena of capsized values,
Let's go treat the doctors, who've been
Infected with administrative negligence!

Let's go vaccinate the nurses, who've been
Laid low by poverty and squalor!
Let's go save the pregnant women
Giving birth on broken beds without mattresses or
*   sheets!*
Let's go pacify the workers, who are
Striking for better working conditions!
Can you see the University Hospital?
That's where you'll find the global disease market!
That's where the sick treat the doctors!
That's where the sick get even sicker!
That's where you can learn to cultivate
Unhealthy habits!*

I still remember the day when I "came home," armed with my certificate in specialist nursing. I was the first woman in my village to have achieved that. After two years of training abroad, with internships in some of the top hospitals, I came back to be of service, to practice my profession. I was ready to pick up the baton, to take over from the expat staff. It was the way the entire country was going. At Independence, the international banks were handing out loans, meaning we suddenly had fully equipped hospitals in our biggest cities. Education and health

---

* Nsah Mala, "Marché mondial des maladies," 2015.

were at the top of the agenda. Our machines were very sophisticated, too sophisticated, in fact. If they broke down, technicians had to be called in from abroad. Local training courses were lagging behind; it was as if the planners in charge of the health system hadn't taken any of these eventualities into account. From one health minister to the next, we encountered the same problems, the same broken promises. Yes, yes, the technical instruments would be fixed as soon as possible. Yes, a rehabilitation program would be put in place, and yes, of course, medical treatment would still be free.

I can't say exactly how it happened. How it was that my colleagues and I slowly, gradually, let our standards slip. We started to compromise. We began turning a blind eye to negligence. We had no choice but to let our patients know there was no more cotton wool, no more alcohol disinfectant, no more syringes, no more suturing thread. It was up to them to buy those things, to send their family members to the nearest pharmacy in order to get what was needed. At the same time, we knew perfectly well just by looking at them that they'd never be able to pay for even half of it. They'd go to the pharmacy, but once they got to the cash register, they'd end up buying just the minimum, or just the cheapest items.

We took to the streets, staging public protests in order to force the government to adopt reforms.

All in vain. Too often, our demands turned into negotiations with our trade union about a salary increase or overtime pay. And, of course, there were some scandals. Money went missing from the health minister's coffers; millions just vanished, stolen from the international aid budget, funds that were earmarked for hospital renovations, for better or more modern equipment, for training more competent staff, for improving hygiene. Government reshuffles all played themselves out in the same way. Each and every new nomination brought new hope, but it never took very long for things to slip back to where they'd been before. How did it happen, for example, that slowly but surely we got used to the fact that senior government officials receive their medical treatment abroad? Isn't that proof that they have no faith in the health system of their own country? These days it seems generally accepted for the President of the Republic to leave the country in his private plane as soon as he feels the slightest twinge of pain. When I finally understood that everything was a sham, I learned to harden myself so that I could continue my work. I could have moved into private medicine, like so many of my colleagues. But no, I never had any doubts about the fact that I would feel more useful working in the public sector, despite my premonition that disaster was about to strike.

———

Nobody was ready when the Ebola outbreak
burst into our lives.

Government ministers talked regularly
about the economic problems our country was
experiencing. They condemned the falling prices of
raw materials on the global markets. They blamed
the repercussions of the war and the ruin of our
infrastructure.

We humans die in a variety of ways. In the fetal
position. With our arms crossed. With our torso
propped up against a wall. Lying flat, our arms
and legs neatly positioned on the bed. While some
of us look perfectly calm, others grimace in pain.
Our heart is a clock whose mechanism we don't
understand. Our veins are blood vessels that can
swell and burst. Our flesh can be destroyed by cells
gone mad.

One day, a poet said to me, "It's no use our
knowing that all paths lead to death, that life is but a
stage, that eternity's the road to nowhere, that Man
must die in order to ripen in the memory of his
descendants; the evidence is nonetheless irrefutable:
Death is not pretty."*

———

* Gabriel Okoundji, *Apprendre à donner, apprendre à recevoir*, 2014

———

However much I resent our failure to get
this crisis under control, we have to admit that our
present needs have grown so great that a solution
seems far out of reach today. Every man and woman
of goodwill, all those who want to assist us, are
welcome. Without exception. They take enormous
risks for our sake. For several months now, I've been
working with volunteers who have come from far
and wide to join us in the struggle. I can see them
battling, unhesitatingly. I can see how much they
give of themselves. I've formed my opinion by being
around them. They're my colleagues, my friends.
When I see solidarity, it makes me want to work
even harder. Because I ask myself, what would the
others think of us if we weren't on the front line?
What one does is never enough. I don't want this
challenge we're facing to defeat us. I want to do my
bit, I want future generations to understand how hard
we fought to stop the triumph of the unacceptable.
We've struggled like soldiers on the battlefield, in
the knowledge that every minute counts. And in the
knowledge, too, that any one of those minutes might
mark the end of our existence. We've done our duty
here on earth.

———

VI

Death accompanies life on its rocky road.
A bridge connects them till the end of time.

When you're fighting Ebola, you can't do anything else. You have to concentrate exclusively on your task. You're focused on the present, and that's it. If you want to survive, you had best not think about anything else. You had best not think about your home, about your normal life. You have to give everything you have; otherwise, the terrible scenes you will witness may completely unhinge you. It's not about you. You're there to defeat the epidemic, and you have your work cut out for you. So you have to leave all your personal problems at home. When burying a body, you need to be as calm as possible. Your mind must be clear.

Some patients are so terrified that they run away at the last minute. The virus attacks the brain to

make its victims more vulnerable. One man left
his bed to lie down next to a woman who had died
during the night. Were they friends? Maybe he didn't
want to go on his journey alone.

When a patient dies, he's immediately
disinfected with chlorine. Then he's placed inside two
plastic body bags. Each bag gets disinfected as well.
Once this is done, he's taken to the morgue. That's the
moment when I can deal with him. We have to wear
masks, plastic suits, goggles, and gloves. There may
be as many as ten in our team, carrying the body on a
stretcher. The graveyard is located directly behind the
treatment center. The soil is reddish and hard.

Toward the end, the man I'm going to bury today
lost his mind. He no longer knew who he was and
what he was doing. He was completely confused.
The path ahead of us has been doused with chlorine.
It makes the grass shiny; one might even say it lights
up our procession. I didn't want to be with the dead,
but that's where I was most urgently needed. After
the epidemic was officially declared, burials were
undertaken by teams from both the government
and the Red Cross. But there was never enough
manpower. Sometimes it took several days before the
bodies were picked up, increasing the risk of infection
for the family members. I heard that staff was being

recruited and trained. When the center opened in this neighborhood, I didn't hesitate, I applied and got the job. My mother didn't approve. I reminded her that I was available because the university had closed. I explained to her that if we young people didn't answer the call, the epidemic would never end. I made it clear that it wasn't because of the money I'd be earning that I had offered my services. I love my country.

Many people say that Ebola is going to kill us all. But be that as it may, I'd rather join the fight than stay in my corner doing nothing. In the end, my mother supported my decision.

Before we lower a body into its freshly dug grave, chlorine is sprayed into the hole and onto the soil all around it. No prayers. No tears. Just a white wooden cross.

Even on the way back, the chlorine sprayer follows us closely. The first time I saw a dead body, it was in such an awful state that I almost quit on the spot. I was told that since I had accepted the job, I was obliged to carry it out. And so I understood that this was a necessary sacrifice. I'm determined to do my duty until the last patient infected with Ebola has left this center, completely cured. In actual fact, I had no idea that the day would come when I would have the courage to take charge of corpses and bury them. I'm an ordinary young guy, I've never looked for specific challenges or tried to show that I was more capable than anybody else. I was rather on the shy side, someone who stayed in the background while others acted.

During the day, the sun fires its scorching rays at us as though it means to punish us. Is that because we keep burying people, sometimes even at night, by generator-produced light? The heat drives me crazy. After half an hour, I can't take it, and my only thought is how to get out of my suit. The plastic traps the heat, it's like a steam room in there. During the burial process, every move I make, however slight, increases the sweating. I have to be extremely careful when lowering a body into its grave with the assistance of my colleagues. A single abrupt gesture, and the bag containing the body begins to leak.

Pouring with sweat and impatient to undress, we return to the center. The hitch is that this, precisely this, is the most dangerous moment. My gloves have touched some of the body fluids, and if I make the smallest error while removing them, I risk contamination.

The chlorine sprayer comes to my aid and helps me disinfect myself completely. I'm reassured by the thought that should I get sick, the doctors will look after me, because I'm one of their own.

Ghosts are what I fear more than anything. The other day, I had to go out and bury a young girl. On the way back, I saw her again. She was blocking my path, so I said to her, "Let me pass, please." When she didn't budge, I asked one of my colleagues to help me, but he replied that he didn't see anybody. Luckily, after a short time, she moved out of the way. I don't understand. I didn't do anything bad. Quite the contrary: we've been instructed in how to bury the dead with dignity. It wasn't I who put an end to their lives. I'm just a helper. Do they want their family members and their friends to become infected as well? Surely not, but they simply can't stop harassing the living who, like me, are tasked with burying their bodies. Actually, they're lost souls, reluctant to leave the earth, hoping we'll help them to return. Their attempts to intimidate us are nothing but distress signals. So if a ghost comes to visit me one of these days—or nights—I simply tell it to leave me alone. Some of the burial teams have to walk a long way to remote villages in order to help the people there bury their dead safely. They show them what they must do and not do; they explain the ways in which things are no longer as they were in the past; and they make it clear that bidding farewell to the deceased according to their traditional customs is no longer allowed.

The key member in each of these teams is the chlorine sprayer. Nothing can happen without him. I get on very well with ours. Although he's older than me, we often go and drink beer together after work. Once, I remember, he was drinking much more than normal. His eyes were bloodshot, and he seemed totally exhausted. Insomnia, he said. I didn't ask him why, I knew the answer already. Just recently, he had been obliged to disinfect the body of one of his childhood friends, someone he used to play soccer with when they were little. As teenagers, they went to the same high school and flirted with the same girls. But his childhood friend's family committed the grave error of keeping his father at home after he fell ill. The whole lot of them got infected. To comfort my colleague, I talk about all sorts of trivial stuff, I make up some harmless jokes. I manage to cheer him up a bit that way. But he's still very upset and keeps repeating, "We've been fighting the virus for months now, and yet I can't really see much progress. Yes, we're putting up resistance, and our common goal unites us, but so far we haven't succeeded in putting a stop to it. Will this war ever end?"

I've spent a lot of time talking to him. He's like a brother to me. I listen very carefully to his words, since whether we live or die really depends on him. He alone can fend off the virus. A warrior in plastic armor. He explains that Ebola is much more resistant than many other viruses: in a contaminated area, it can remain active for two weeks or more. "Do you realize what that means?" he asks. "This is the reason why I have to be vigilant at all times. If I lose my concentration for a single moment, it could be fatal. Every day I have to start all over again with the spraying and the disinfecting. The chlorine solution is my best friend. It knows where Ebola is hiding. It can see it easily, whereas for us humans, it's invisible. Our eyes aren't strong enough to detect it. Yes, chlorine really is my best friend. I know everything about it. It's the chemical element with the atomic number 17 and the symbol Cl, and it's the most common halogen. It's a yellow gas with tinges of green. It has a much higher density than air. It gives off a suffocating odor and is very toxic."

I have seen the sprayer use his apparatus with great skill and precision, ensuring that all surfaces are evenly covered and not a single little corner is left out. With his wand, he disinfects the tents, the treatment rooms, the toilets, the garbage bins, the ambulances, the suits, and the corpses. He disinfects everything that Ebola has touched. When he has to go inside the houses of the sick, he sprays the walls, the furniture, and the floor. He picks up objects that are lying around. No one likes to see him. He never looks anyone in the eye when he arrives to do his spraying, because he's too afraid of detecting the confusion, the fear, and the hatred he inspires. Sometimes he's no longer sure whether he's working for or against society. He has repeatedly told me that he just wants to get back to the land and plant yams, manioc, and red tomatoes.

I hear him muttering that he's lost his illusions.
One morning, he went into a house. For days, a
young girl had been waiting there for someone to
come and remove her parents' bodies. They were
lying lifeless in the empty house. She had called
the emergency number many times, asking for an
ambulance to come and pick them up. But no one
came. All the ambulances were busy. She'd kept
calling them, again and again. By the time the
emergency team finally got there, the young girl was
in a state of extreme distress and feeling ill. It was too
late; she was already infected.

There are no certainties. We were so sure that
all we had to do to defeat Ebola was join forces.
But the sprayer is right. The virus takes a few steps
backward only so it can charge forward even harder.
I envy the people who live elsewhere, far away from
this country. They can still believe in happiness.
They make plans for their future and that of their
children. Their sleep is undisturbed by nightmares.
I envy those lucky enough to find a certain measure
of fulfillment in their lives. For them, obstacles aren't
insurmountable.

What saddens me most of all is the utter
humiliation of the sick in the face of death. They
become unrecognizable, they lose their identity and
their past. And yet, they've been loved, and they
themselves have loved. I've seen many of them,

emaciated bodies that Ebola already had in its grip. Nothing human was left of them. I've realized that we're born with a "reverse calendar" inside us. Like a ticking clock that counts the number of our days on earth—but backwards. How I wish I knew who winds up that clock! Because I myself can see no logic in all this horror. I've never been enthusiastic about churchgoing. Even when I was small, my mother didn't take me along because I asked too many embarrassing questions. All I know is that my brother goes to mass—but he has steadfastly refused to work at the center. He prefers listening to what the priest tells the believers: "Ebola is Evil incarnate. It has come to punish you for your sins. Those who have stopped following God's Word will perish; the rest have nothing to fear."

If only my brother understood the importance of what we do! When all the precautions are precisely followed at a burial, for example, no one catches the disease.

During our training, we were told the story of a female traditional healer who was so famous that people from all over the region came to see her. She knew where to find the best medicinal herbs in the forest, and she knew how to prepare the most effective remedies. It was said that her hands had extraordinary healing power when she laid them on a sick person's body. And yet, despite all her

knowledge, this woman didn't suspect the danger
that lay in store for her. Or maybe she was aware
of it, but still she absolutely wanted to find a cure
for this disease. She caught Ebola from one of her
patients and died of it. Hundreds of mourners came
from far and wide to attend her funeral. Wanting to
pay their last respects, the procession accompanied
her mortal remains all the way to the grave. Today,
experts estimate that this funeral was responsible for
over three hundred deaths. It really taught us a lesson.
At the same time, it hasn't prevented people from
trying to bury their dead with a measure of dignity.
So, since we don't want them to hide their dead
or refuse to hand them over to us, we're prepared
to make some concessions. If the family insists on
having the body placed in a coffin, we don't oppose
it. If they provide ceremonial garments to clothe the
deceased, we respect their wishes. And if the relatives
want to come to the cemetery, we just ask them to
keep a four-meter distance. There are those who
want to dig the grave with their own hands, and
there's no reason whatsoever for not allowing that.
We explain the procedure to them. All we really
want from them is their cooperation.

It will take years for us to recover from what
we've lived through. And also to forget. I tell myself
that life is incomprehensible. We need death to bring
us back together.

VII

A mother's love carries death away on its wings
across a turbulent sky.

A mother is dying. Her body is giving up on her, and the end is near. Her spirit is dispersing. It collides with the walls of her house and tries to dissolve into space. The mother is scared, she'd rather stay in her narrow little world. She wouldn't ask for much: the flowers in her garden, the song of a bird on her windowsill, or her cat's soft fur. She doesn't want to leave her house, where every nook and cranny is familiar. The walls talk to her. The furniture knows all about her. The pieces bear the imprint of those former days when she was happy, or to be more precise, when she could live a worry-free life. Her thoughts are engraved in the house's bricks and mortar. It's imbued with her scent. Just go inside

and her presence is everywhere, from the carpet to
the ornaments. Everything is reminiscent of her.

She wants to die here, at home. Close the door
and turn the key twice, she says. Board up the
windows if you like, but I'm staying put. I want to
die in my own bed. Burn down the house if you
must, but please leave me in peace! I refuse to spend
my final days among the sick and dying. This is the
house I shared with my husband. This is the house
where my children grew up. All my memories,
both good and bad, are here. The separation. The
divorce. The quarrels. The yelling in front of our
three sons, who were in tears. But it's also where
we used to make love, so passionately, right here
in this bed. New life was conceived between these
very sheets. And when our boys were born, I
nursed them in this bed, letting their greedy little
mouths suckle my breasts. While I was raising my
children, I never refused them anything. My life as
a woman may have been solitary at times, it is true,
but there was always an abundance of affection.
When we all went out together, I couldn't help
smiling, I was so proud of having brought them
into the world.

Children shouldn't have to die before their
parents. It's against the law of nature. They ought to
stay near their parents and look after them in their
old age, listen to them, bring them food and do their

laundry for them. They ought to offer them the
tenderness they miss so much when life gets hard
and each step requires a superhuman effort and each
breath hurts and their heart is in free fall.

A mother shouldn't have to witness the death
of her children. Her eyes shouldn't have to gaze
upon their mortal remains; she shouldn't have to
watch those she carried in her belly die while she is
powerless to bring them back to life all over again. I
was prepared to give up my body for them like the
first time, when they floated inside me, drawing their
sustenance from my womb. I tried my hardest to
nurse them back to health.

A mother shouldn't have to watch her children
growing weaker, more and more lethargic, losing
blood, when she has no way to stop the hemorrhage.
We were a close-knit family, despite our problems.
The oldest was rather shy and introverted, but he
always cared for others. The second one, on the other
hand, was jolly and full of mischief. And the last
one, still small, got showered with his older brothers'
love and affection. When he fell ill, they dropped
everything and hurried home to help me look after
him. Yes, we were a close-knit family. I never felt
lonely. I was a very happy mother.

Ebola hits out blindly. It stabs you in the back
without mercy. What mysterious force guides its
hand? A brutal, ruthless force.

Long ago, God decided to let human beings live
and die without His intervention. In His infinite
magnitude, the tribulations of our existence don't
touch him. Those who implore His pity are mistaken.
He owns the oceans, the earth, the sky, and everything
touched by light. He looks upon humanity with
irritation. Rather a failed experiment, isn't it? It will
take Him another eternity to come up with a better
design. In the meanwhile, He races across Time, from
beginning to end, in search of inspiration. Sometimes
He goes to sleep at the back of the sun and forgets
who we are. His sleep is infinite. God is bored, and
His boredom is frightening. He's blind; His empty
pupils pierce our conscience. He's mute; His outcry
penetrates our bodies. He's unique; His solitude
pervades the entire universe.

From fluorescent anemones to the Himalayan
mountains, nothing can equal the splendor of His
creation. With infinite generosity and tenderness,
He thought of everything. But He got nothing in
exchange. Or very little, and so He felt betrayed.
Now He's indifferent to everything and so weary that
He's tired of eternity. To be eternal is exactly what
He doesn't want anymore. How to love without end?
How to be happy without having experienced sorrow?

Let me die here, in my own house! I want my
house to be my shroud, I want the walls to cave in
and guard the secret of our death rattles. I've called

out to God in vain. So now I am turning to you, Mother Mary. You alone know what separation means, absence, the impossibility of changing the world. You alone can comprehend my suffering. When you were giving birth, parts of the placenta and the remainder of the afterbirth were expelled from your belly. Blood spurted out. My blood is red, like yours. I am a woman like you; like yours, my sex needed to expand to allow the child to come out.

I am confiding in you, Mother Mary. Take me in your arms and cradle my pain. I shall follow you all the way to the end of your suffering.

You suffered the pain of witnessing your son's cruel death. When you found that the body had disappeared, you refused to believe it and stood on the threshold of the empty tomb. I know your story by heart. I keep the Bible by my side. All my life, like a beacon in the night. Your pain goes like this:

Early on Sunday, while it was still dark, Mary Magdalene went to the tomb and saw that the stone had been removed from the entrance. So she came running to Simon Peter and the other disciple, the one Jesus loved, and said: "They have removed the Lord out of the tomb and we don't know where they have put him!"

So Peter and the other disciple started for the tomb. Both were running, but the other disciple outran Peter and reached the tomb first. He bent over and looked in at the strips of linen lying there, but did not go in. Then Simon Peter came along behind him and went straight into the tomb. He saw the strips of linen, as well as the cloth that had been wrapped around Jesus's head. The cloth was not with the linen, but rolled up and left elsewhere. Finally the other disciple, who had reached the tomb first, also went inside. He saw and believed. They still did not understand from Scripture that Jesus had to rise from the dead. Then the disciples went back to where they were staying.

Now Mary stood outside the tomb crying. As she wept, she bent over to look into the tomb and saw two angels in white, seated where Jesus's body had been, one at the head and the other at the foot. They asked her, "Woman, why are you crying?"

"They have taken my Lord away," she said, "and I don't know where they have put him." At this, she turned around and saw Jesus standing there, but she did not realize that it was Jesus.

He asked her, "Woman, why are you crying? Who is it you are looking for?"

Thinking he was the gardener, she said, "Sir, if you have carried him away, tell me where you have put him, and I will get him."

Jesus said to her, "Mary." She turned toward him and cried out in Hebrew, "Rabbouni!" which means teacher. Jesus said, "Do not hold on to me, for I have not yet ascended to the Father. Go instead to my brothers and tell them that I am ascending to my Father and your Father, to my God and your God."

*Mary Magdalene went to the disciples with the news
that she had seen the Lord and that he had said these things
to her.**

I believe in you, Mother Mary. You who are so
close to us, help me accept that my sons have taken
the lighted path, and are finally relieved of their
earthly sufferings.

I can taste blood in my mouth. My mind is
drifting, my body dissolving. The pain binds me to
my children like an umbilical cord.

But over there, in the distance, an ambulance
siren sends out a wail that shreds the fabric of the day.
Pedestrians in the streets of the city disperse rapidly
as the vehicle approaches, and then they watch in
terror to see where it's headed. They know that death
moves quickly, looking for bodies.

All of a sudden, the emergency team arrives at the
house. A sharp kick, and the bedroom door opens
noisily. The stinging odor of chlorine fills the air.
Men in spacesuits are already bending down over the
mother.

---

* John 20:1–18.

VIII

When surviving is more painful than living and
your sorrow is that you still walk the earth.

My father said to me, "Go on, get out now. Go to the capital, go to your aunt. The village is cursed. Don't ever come back here." I stuffed some clothes into a bag and took the money he was holding out to me. I knew it was all he had left. When the bus arrived at the main station, my aunt was there, waiting for me. After we got to her house, I cried a lot. I withdrew into a corner and exchanged a few words with my cousins from time to time, but I refused to go out. A few days later, my body started to itch. I had the feeling that something had gotten into my blood. My heart wasn't the same as before, it seemed too tired to keep on beating. After the slightest exertion, I was out of breath. Next, I got a terrible stomachache. My aunt didn't know what was the matter with me.

Finally, one day the Ministry of Health released a statement that was broadcast on radio and TV and published in all the newspapers. It informed the population about the outbreak of a disease that typically carries a high mortality rate: "The samples that were sent to France for analysis at the Pasteur Institute have tested positive for the Ebola virus (species *Zaire ebolavirus*)," it said. "These cases have been reported in three regions in the southeast of the country, as well as in certain parts of the capital. In addition, several neighboring countries have also reported a number of cases of the disease on their territory. As a result, we will take whatever measures are necessary to halt the outbreak of this virus. We are appealing to the population to follow the hygiene instructions. From now on, the consumption of bushmeat is prohibited. Violations of this rule will be punished with hard prison time. Hands must be washed with diluted bleach. As soon as any symptoms appear, you have to go immediately to the nearest hospital. Stay vigilant. Stay calm. A state of emergency has been declared throughout the nation."

Panic seized the population. In every neighborhood, the blare of ambulance sirens could be heard. People suspected of having the disease were arrested. Others who were actually infected would collapse in the street, and no one went near them. The health minister organized recovery teams to collect the bodies, but the response time simply wasn't quick enough. Media reports talked about nothing but the disease.

My aunt immediately became suspicious about me. She called the central number and asked for an ambulance to come and pick me up. After I arrived at the hospital, my test results were positive. I was admitted to a wing of the building reserved for Ebola patients. For a month and a day, my body hovered between life and death. I was bleeding from the nose, vomiting blood, suffering atrociously. The chaos all around me was horrendous, while the medical staff was on the verge of despair. Every corpse left behind puddles of bodily fluids—blood, phlegm, and other secretions. There was hardly enough time to clean up the traces of death before someone else was brought in...I've seen nurses doing their work without any protection, even though the floor was soiled with vomit and excrement. No one wanted to come near us, so scraps of food were thrown to us from a distance. There were so many dead that the bodies were piled up in a dark room; some had been tossed there headfirst, while others lay with their legs spread apart, repulsive in their nakedness.

How did I survive? Why was I singled out, despite being no better than any of the others? I heard the sick howling in their dread of the gruesome end that awaited them. They didn't understand. Why, after leading such good, decent lives, could they not expect to be saved?

I recovered, thanks to the efforts of the caregivers who gave their all in the battle to expel Ebola from my body. I shall be grateful to them for the rest of my life. But being admitted to a hospital is like entering some kind of underworld. Everything goes dark. You become disorientated. There's nothing left except inside and outside. Time's your master, its power is absolute, and you must submit. You must wait for your organism to recover its balance and regain the place it lost.

Often, I would look out the window at the huge, majestic tree in the courtyard. The tree put me in mind of the baobab of my childhood. Sometimes, very early in the morning, I heard the birds chirping in its foliage. I found it very beautiful, and its presence gave me strength.

Slowly, ever so slowly, I began to respond to the rehydration therapy. My body started working again. I was able to leave my bed and walk around. Taking small, cautious steps. Later, I paid the tree a visit, to thank it for comforting us in the depths of our despair. When I leaned against it, I could sense its life-giving vibrations. I pressed my ear against its rough bark, and it spoke to me, whispering that it was there for me. I hugged it again and again.

I was tested at intervals of several days. All the results were negative. Then the doctor declared, "You've made it, you're free to leave!" I washed myself with chlorinated water and was given clean new clothes, since my old ones had all been incinerated on the day I arrived. To help me gain strength, I also received a kit containing some protein-rich food and some vitamins.

When I tried to enter my aunt's house, she refused to take me back. Two of my cousins had fallen ill, and she blamed me. I had no choice but to return to the hospital, where I was put up in a dormitory reserved for patients' families who didn't want to leave their sick relative alone or who had nowhere to go. There were posters on the walls warning that the establishment would soon be closed down. The patients were going to be transferred to special Ebola clinics that were being set up all over the country. They were looking for volunteers, and then a nurse came to see me. She suggested I should get involved, since the virus no longer posed any danger to me. I had survived, and now I was immunized for life. It couldn't hurt me anymore. She said that because I was young, I would be the ideal person to counsel patients of my own age. I hesitated for a long time. And then I thought about my parents and my brothers, who, my aunt had informed me, were all dead. Still aching from the pain of not having been able to do anything to help them, I told myself that this was my chance to make up for that failure. So I said yes, and I was assigned to one of the new treatment centers.

When young patients are brought in, I'm the one who receives them. If I see that they're losing hope and saying they're about to die, I tell them that they, too, can survive as I did. They have to realize that it's possible. I know very well how they must be feeling, lying there in their beds, all alone. They have the impression that an unknown force has taken control of their existence. They don't know how to defend themselves. It's a feeling I wouldn't wish on my worst enemy. I try to encourage them. I tell them that anyone can catch this disease, that it's not their fault. I make it clear to them that they must never stop fighting, even when they feel their strength giving out.

I belong to a group of female Ebola survivors. We go around the town, explaining that people like us still have their rightful place in the community. We present no risk, we say, and we shouldn't be ostracized. We choose our words carefully and try to be reassuring. Generally, we're accompanied by women who have never had the virus themselves. We hold one another by the hand, we walk side by side, and we talk among ourselves, showing the others that there's nothing to fear.

Yes, it's true, I was lucky to escape with my life. But deep down I can't help thinking that I wasn't the one who should have been spared. The man who should have survived at all costs was our head physician, who was personally responsible for the recovery of hundreds of patients. He was the only hemorrhagic-fever specialist in the entire country. We were all praying, but in vain, he couldn't be saved. All the newspapers carried articles about his death.

I read that one day, at the Ebola center he'd been running for many months, he told one of his colleagues that he wasn't feeling well. He'd done his regular patient rounds that same morning. On seeing a male nurse who had contracted the virus and was now lying among the other patients, the doctor had said to him, "But, my son, what are you doing here?" He didn't know that it would soon be his turn. The center was full, and the sick were everywhere, even on mats laid out on the floor. He didn't want to stop, or maybe he just couldn't stop. But before long, he started shivering and he was forced to take a few days off to rest. It turned out that it wasn't just a bout of malaria; it was actually Ebola.

His colleagues immediately went into action. They put in a request at the local branch of a large health organization to have him urgently evacuated to Europe. "No," the answer came back, "because the head physician is not a member of our staff." A petition was circulated, calling on the international community to have him taken to the United States or Great Britain for treatment. All in vain.

Some Canadian researchers who were working at a local laboratory had a small supply of an experimental treatment. This "secret serum" had been shown to be effective in monkeys infected with Ebola. So far, it had never been tried on humans, but at least it offered a chance of saving him. Unfortunately, he had been transferred to another treatment center. Contrary to all expectations, the people in charge of that center replied that in good conscience they felt it would be unfair to give him the serum, since there were so many other patients who needed it just as much as he did. And besides, they didn't agree with the idea of administering experimental treatments with unknown effects that might even turn out to be negative in the long run. Time passed, and his health deteriorated.

Finally, after countless discussions and negotiations, his evacuation abroad was authorized. But it couldn't be carried out because of his vomiting,

which made moving him extremely dangerous.
While attempts were made to solve this problem,
more time passed, and he died a few days later.

The whole country was profoundly shaken. For
the first time, Ebola was no longer anonymous. It
had a well-known face. A young doctor commenting
on this on the radio explained that the impact of this
death reached far beyond our national borders. He
discussed the enormous disparities regarding access
to treatment and talked about the indifference and
institutional inertia that reigned in the Department
of Health. In a Western country, a senior politician
made the following statement: "Globalization brings
us closer to our African fellow citizens, while the
media have the opposite effect. Another alienating
factor is our widespread indifference toward the
terrible crisis into which these countries have
been plunged. Any active involvement, be it at the
international, national, community, or even personal
level, seems to stop at the borders, at the barriers
everyone's putting up."

We needed our doctor's courage so much! We
needed his example so much! He wasn't the only one
who died that way.

We, survivors of the epidemic, suffer in silence.
We carry invisible, painful scars. We want to lead
normal lives, but the stigma of the virus keeps us
apart from other people. In my village, my family

home was burned down; all that's left of it is dry wood and ashes.

The other day it rained. That made me happy. Rain, finally. I went outside so that the rain would touch my body. So that every drop would clean my face and tell me that rebirth was still possible.

IX

It's not the uniform that makes the man;
it's circumstances that reveal his noble heart.

I'm a prefect, in charge of the outreach teams that
are currently visiting my part of the country.
Their brief is to explain at length. They give
detailed information about the illness: its mode of
transmission, the risks, the available treatments. They
must stress the need for people to go straight to a
treatment center at the first sign of symptoms. In
certain cases, people will be placed under quarantine.
The teams have to go over the strict safety
regulations again and again.

Science alone is not enough to bring the virus
under control. We need so much more than that. We
need to reduce the level of ignorance. The tension.
The fear. Human beings are not just vectors of
infection. All that callousness is contraindicated. All

that cold, scientific reasoning just undermines our efforts.

That's why I keep telling my teams that they have to practice the art of persuasion. They must convince people that they should stop visiting the sick, and that dropping in on patients' families and friends to support them in their ordeal is now out of the question.

The sick woman is slumped in her armchair. Her clothes are creased, her braids undone. She looks bad, and her hands are trembling. There are a lot of people milling around. Young girls are busy in the kitchen, cooking porridge. In one of the corners of the house, children are playing. The boy is her son, and the little girl belongs to the neighbors. She's only eighteen months old and wanders around among the adults, holding on to them. The sick woman's husband is in the bedroom. He's not well either. His sisters, come to take care of the household, are cleaning the house. No one knows that the disease has staked out its territory and will gain ground at great speed. Before much time passes, not many of these visitors will be left alive. But from time immemorial, solidarity has been expressed in this way. It was like that in the villages, and also in the working-class neighborhoods in the town. "If I help you out today, you'll lend me a hand tomorrow"—that makes them stronger, and it's how they were brought up. Rejoicing together, weeping together. You show compassion, give some money for medicine, or bring along a few soft drinks. It's the gesture that counts.

My outreach units are tasked with explaining that this way of life has to end, that shaking hands, touching, embracing one another are no longer allowed. Instead, you have to keep your distance from other people, stay at home, and wash your hands with disinfectant before entering a public space.

The teams emphasize that, even if a person doesn't show any suspicious signs, he or she may already be infected. And, as soon as they get sick, they remain contagious for several weeks—including after their death. As a matter of fact, the corpse is more dangerous than anything else. Above all, don't touch it. Ebola kills a very high percentage of those afflicted, and there's no medication that can change that!

In order to reassure the population, the outreach units also say that this virus is not new. The doctors know a lot about it, such as the way it spreads, or the protective measures one needs to take against it. They know you can't catch it just by breathing, which is good news.

The outreach teams have to exercise patience. They need to find the right words. Because when people are afraid, they will act irrationally. The contradictory claims and rumors going around

about Ebola create a lot of uncertainty in peoples'
minds. The rate at which it spreads, its virulence,
that's all too much to grasp, and very hard to accept.
Sometimes it's just easier to lie to yourself. It's easier
simply to disbelieve the evidence before your eyes,
in your own village, in your own neighborhood.
Despite the public notices, many prefer to hide the
sick, or even, if the threat becomes real, to die with
them. What's the point, they say, it was a losing game
right from the start. The most vulnerable members
of society, women and children, have to bow to the
decrees of the elders. They're excluded from the
discussions, and thus they have no inkling of the
dangers lying in wait for them.

The outreach teams have to strike the right note.

I also send other units to the remote areas, in
four-wheel-drive vehicles donated by a humanitarian
organization. The units distribute kits for protecting
the whole family and for disinfecting the house.
Whenever one of these teams approaches a village
where Ebola cases have been reported, the members
are well aware of the risks they're taking. They
arrive wearing heavy rubber boots and dressed in
the official uniform. They avoid touching anything.
They keep their distance. And while handing out
color brochures that explain the virus and its modes
of transmission, they keep their hands protected with
gloves. Sometimes people just shrug when they're

told to stop eating bushmeat. "That doesn't make sense," they reply. "How are we going to feed ourselves now?"

The outreach teams know not to respond to mockery. In every village throughout the region, they spend entire days talking to the people and making them understand that these measures won't last forever, but only until this terrible disease disappears. The people aren't convinced. They say, "You're telling us that if we get sick, we need to go to an Ebola clinic right away. But at the same time, you yourselves also tell us that there's no treatment. So what is it you're actually trying to say?"

In this ruthless war against Ebola, words are very powerful weapons. Or at any rate, that's what I'd like to believe. But there are still many problems to be dealt with. Why is it that, in the middle of such an epidemic, hundreds of public health officials feel they must clamor for indemnity payments and threaten to go on strike? They want financial compensation for the risks they're taking; they want assurance that their families will be looked after in the event that they die from Ebola. I have personally promised that I'll try to move heaven and earth for them.

It's true that a lot of money is changing hands in these critical times. It would have been better if the international community hadn't publicly announced how much money has been donated for humanitarian aid. The amounts sound like colossal sums, but that creates a false idea of the situation. The economy is collapsing. Economic activity has come to a halt. Trade with neighboring countries has stopped, the borders are closed, infrastructure projects have been postponed. Most airline companies have canceled their flights. The tourists have all gone, and the schools and universities are closed. Shops and markets are deserted. Farmers have stopped tending their fields. Normal, everyday illnesses are ignored, medicines have run out. All medical treatments for other health conditions have been suspended overnight. If someone collapses in the street from a heart attack, nobody will go near him. He's left there unaided until an ambulance comes and takes him to an Ebola center, which is the very place where he shouldn't be. Pregnant women can't find anywhere to give birth.

Ebola! Ebola! Ebola!

And yet, for the first few months, the epidemic was underestimated. Fundraising efforts were slow. Instead of inspiring compassion and support, the increased media coverage caused the opposite reaction: self-preservation and withdrawal.

Infectious disease experts were well aware that the Ebola virus existed, but they thought it would behave as usual. They expected a very localized outbreak that would be over once it had claimed a few dozen victims. Since the virus was identified in 1976, hadn't there been something like twenty outbreaks, but hadn't they all been relatively mild? Only as time went by did they realize how wrong they were. The virus had changed tactics. It had left the forest and moved into the urban areas, where population density and mobility were much greater. When they saw what was happening, the local NGOs rang the alarm bells: we need to act fast! They were shocked by the lack of reaction, claiming that if this crisis had struck any other region on the globe, it would have been dealt with differently.

But it was already too late—the epidemic was out of control. The virus was on the move in three different countries, and threatened to travel even farther afield. And it was at that moment that the first cases of infection were reported in the West. The media were going mad; the international community was in turmoil. A Spanish priest who became infected at an Ebola treatment center was repatriated in a hurry. He died of the virus in Spain. Some months later, another missionary died in a hospital in Madrid, having passed on the virus to one of the assistant nurses who had cared for him. At the same time, an African traveler fell ill in the United States and died just a few days after his arrival, having infected two nurses. The apprehension reached a fever pitch when the Americans found out that the second nurse, after treating the patient, had taken a plane. The public health authorities were now forced to trace the 132 passengers who had traveled with her and who had to be put under observation. The world was now fully aware of the extent of the danger. Just how far was this epidemic going to spread? How long would it last? The possibility of a globalized Ebola outbreak was fostering panic.

The countries of the West realized how vulnerable they were. Health checks at the point of arrival for all flights coming from the affected geographical areas were put in place at most airports. And there were checks at departure too. Travelers had their temperature taken, there were forms to fill in, suspect passengers were placed in isolation.

Right then, what we most urgently needed was money! International aid was doubled, then tripled. Quadrupled. Western heads of state decided to hold a summit. Its goal was to develop a plan of action to bring the crisis under control. The UN Security Council set up an emergency committee exclusively dedicated to the fight against Ebola. The organization demanded that its member states "dramatically accelerate and expand their financial and material support."

The result was mobilization on every continent, with the participation of numerous sectors of the economy, both public and private. Billions of dollars were said to be in play. But there was still a lack of funds, and the virus continued to spread. Experts declared: "The epidemic has left us far behind; it's making headway much faster than we are, and it's about to win the race..."

The American president now proposed a much more aggressive response: war! Military troops were deployed. The other countries followed, particularly France and Great Britain. The soldiers were trained in combat, skilled in confronting an invisible, highly dangerous enemy, capable of exercising crowd control and securing high-risk zones. They had to transport equipment and construct new treatment centers. They were responsible for the recruitment of staff and the intensive training of health workers. It was a massive offensive. A fierce onslaught that required sharing strategic and medical information among all the participating countries.

The idea was that the military was needed to beat the virus into retreat. However, if I, as someone on the ground, were asked to make a comment, I would address the international community. I'd tell them that fear can provoke a strong reaction, which will in turn free up enormous resources and placate public opinion. But the outcome will not necessarily be the best in the long run. True solidarity is meant to be durable. And in that respect, if I may offer the international community a further piece of advice, I would ask them to investigate how the aid payments were managed. Have the infrastructure rehabilitation projects actually been implemented? Has staff training been effective? Are we better prepared if disaster strikes again, or has everything fallen into oblivion already, crowded out by the thick bustle of our days?

X

*When the specter of death sows discord
among humans, don't look away.*

It was during my stint as a volunteer abroad,
working for an NGO at a treatment center in
a remote region, that I became infected with the
Ebola virus. I was immediately transferred to the
capital, where a medical team was waiting for me.
Preparations were made for my repatriation. I was
placed in a transparent plastic tent, under negative air
pressure and strict security: a kind of mobile isolation
chamber. An airplane specially equipped with an
"Aeromedical Biological Containment System," used
for patients with highly contagious diseases, stood
at the back of the runway. Once my tent had been
set up, the plane took off. And with me was a whole
medical team. The journey home was long; it gave
me a chance to look back on my life. My desire to go

to Africa, and my wish to serve in a country where
so much remains to be done. I'd found a humanity
there that made me question my outlook on life. It
also made me more humble. But lying in that bubble,
I couldn't stop thinking of the inferno I had just left
behind.

On landing, an ambulance, forming a convoy
with a number of other vehicles, took me to a
hospital with a special wing for infectious diseases.
Dressed in a protective suit, and helped by one of my
attendants, I entered the building. I was very lucky.
Most relief organizations refuse to take on patients
as contagious as I was. Is it acceptable to repatriate
someone who's extremely likely to infect the people
around him? If so, under what conditions? And if
not, how do you justify such a refusal, and do you
think that from then on, even a single volunteer
would still be prepared to risk his life?

The diagnosis was shocking: severe organ failure.
I was admitted to the reanimation ward.

Several weeks later, from my isolation chamber,
I made the following televised declaration: "To all
those who are lending me support and have sent me
good wishes for my recovery, I would like to say that
I'm receiving the best treatment possible. I'm steadily
getting stronger. I've had the privilege of working
in Africa for many years. When the Ebola outbreak
was made public, I wanted to be involved in the fight

against this dreadful virus. I've seen devastation and death. I still remember each face and every name. Thank you for your prayers. May God help us in these times of great uncertainty."

I left the hospital officially cured, after more than a month in intensive care combined with an experimental treatment. The press conference that was held on the occasion attracted a large number of journalists. I had my wife and children by my side.

Science had won!

Several months went by without incident. But then, one day, I started feeling unwell again, and I had to return to the hospital where I had been admitted the first time. The doctors discovered that Ebola had not been completely eradicated from my body. The test results showed that the virus had lodged itself in my left eye. Before I had the disease, my iris had been blue, but afterwards it turned green. Ebola had gone into hiding where no one would expect to find it. Inside an organ that my immune system could not easily access.

It was news to me that such sequelae were quite common among Ebola survivors. Secondary effects include backache, tendonitis, a crawling sensation in the legs, eye inflammations potentially leading to blindness, extreme fatigue, and cognitive difficulties. Ebola manages to hide in the joints, the spinal cord, the testicles, the sperm, and possibly also in vaginal secretions. This means that humans, too, have become reservoirs for the virus! So far, nobody knows whether this will pass or whether we are in this for the long term.

The history of Ebola is punctuated with speculations, questionings, incomplete answers, and a whole lot of theories.

I had already been evacuated when quarantine was adopted as a general strategy in the country I had just left. Never could I have imagined that the day would come when men, women, and children would be treated like lepers and kept incarcerated by force in their own homes.

On government order, policemen and soldiers in combat uniform were blocking off entrance and exit doors. The slum-dwellers woke up with a start. They'd just learned that they were locked in, imprisoned, exiled. Strictly forbidden to go beyond the boundaries of the shantytown where they'd spent their entire lives. A wretched place with open sewers, a nauseating stench, and garbage that had piled up for years, because no one had bothered to remove it. Illegal electricity connections, with cables trailing on the ground. Community wells, where the women would go and fetch water in large plastic tubs, metal containers, and buckets that they kept inside their shacks. Overcrowded schools, where the kids had to squeeze onto rickety benches set in front of shabby old blackboards. Teachers who were overwhelmed by the enormity of their task. Not a single hospital far and wide, only run-down dispensaries and private clinics, eager to cash in on bogus cures. Women walked from compound to compound bearing trays on their heads, trays loaded with pills and tablets for sale, medications that were either expired or of questionable provenance.

The inhabitants of the shantytown were told they could no longer come and go as they pleased. "We want to protect the part of the population that's not infected. Food, medical supplies, and essential items will be handed out to you," an official voice cried through a loudspeaker.

People were angry. Groups of young men armed with stones and sticks tried to rip out the barbed wire that had been put up during the night and was blocking their passage. They wanted to run away. The soldiers took aim and fired into the crowd, which started to back away. A teenaged boy cringed with pain and grasped his injured leg. A bullet had pierced his flesh and shattered the bone. *Help me!* In the chaos and fury that engulfed the place, no one came to his aid.

A few weeks earlier, an isolation center that had opened in the same part of town was ransacked and the patients turned out. The generator, food, mattresses, and bloodstained sheets were carried off with no inkling that they were infectious. Tear gas was used to disperse the looters. The government imposed an immediate curfew; the president issued a warning to the rioting crowds. He made threats, explained that the situation was very serious and that national security was at stake. Anarchy had to be stopped by any means necessary.

Will future outbreaks—and they will inevitably occur—strike the villages in the forest, or the big cities? Are we aware that this isn't the end, but only the beginning of a lengthy battle?

XI

Orphaned children are like celestial bodies
whose orbits lie far from the sun.

I'm looking at the small boy who has fallen asleep
from sheer exhaustion, asking myself what will
become of the orphans left behind by Ebola. At the
age of seven, he has spent months wandering around
the streets of the capital, not knowing where to go.
Months of living on scraps of food, or eating nothing
at all for days on end. Months of sleeping in the dust.
And yet, he is a miracle child. Even though he stayed
at home with his parents, both of whom had the
disease, he didn't get infected.

I read in a magazine that Ebola is particularly
virulent in children. The younger they are, the
weaker their immune system tends to be, and thus
the more vulnerable they are. Furthermore—
strangely enough—the incubation period is only half

of what it is for adults. I feel great pity looking at
this child who had to watch helplessly as his father
and mother died. When the burial team, alerted
by the neighbors, came to collect the bodies, he
hid in the kitchen. Through the partially open
door, he watched the men pick up the corpses after
drenching them with disinfectant. Suddenly, the air
was permeated by an overpowering smell, a smell
that would stay fixed in his memory forever. When
at last he came out of his hiding place, very early
the following morning, no one wanted anything to
do with him. The neighbors didn't let him come
near them and told him to leave the area. "Get away
from here," one of them yelled. "We don't want to
get infected!" Since Ebola had invaded his family,
everyone thought he must be carrying the virus
inside his body. Fear prevailed over compassion.
I'm convinced that before, he would have been
immediately taken in by the neighbors until relatives
came to fetch him. But under the circumstances, the
street became his refuge. What sort of a refuge? For
a long time, he was completely alone; then he joined
some other children who'd been cast out like himself,
marginalized, avoided by the passersby. The children
resorted to scavenging in the dustbins, or to petty
theft, in the knowledge that nobody would run after
them. It was only toward the end of the epidemic
that members of a humanitarian organization found

him wandering around aimlessly in the backstreets
of the city. They took him and some of the other
boys to a provisional reception center. There, he was
offered a semblance of normality, a calming routine.
He could play with the other children, and there was
storytelling, guessing games, and singing contests.
What was important to the charity workers was to
see the kids smile again, to offer them distractions
from thinking too much about the loved ones they
had lost.

Thanks to its family reunification network, the
reception center was able to track me down. One
day, some men came knocking at our door. They
explained that they were looking for a new home for
the little one. I'm just a distant relative on his paternal
side, but that's irrelevant, since in our culture, the
degree of proximity of the family ties basically
doesn't count. The men said there was nothing to
fear, since a whole year after his parents' death, he
had remained untouched by the illness. So I said
yes. I had some problems with my daughter and her
husband, who have two young sons and a baby girl.
Initially, they were against it. But on the other hand,
everyone understood that we had to keep trying to
do our part. Ebola is about that too . . . To help us
financially to take him on, they promised us social

aid money, and we also received a single mattress, some sheets, food supplies, some clothes and shoes, as well as some tableware.

The child calls me "Grandmother." That's what I'd like to be to him. But, since he came to live with us ten days ago, I've been wondering what his future may hold. I'm not just worried for him, but for all young children who've had to experience the epidemic. Maybe they're not all orphans, but what they had to go through—the dreadful scenes, the palpable fear—has left them deeply scarred. They've lost their innocence. They've lost the kingdom of their childhood. They've learned that their parents aren't immortal, that life can turn upside down from one day to the next. They're just kids, but they're already old. Can they hope ever to live a life free of the fear that the horror will return?

Ebola has touched the lives of so many children! And let's not forget about those who were infected and survived. Some of them are now heads of a household, which means they alone are looking after their younger brothers and sisters in the ruins of their home. They have nothing else left. They're called "Ebola children."

Before falling asleep one night, the boy asked me whether he could go back to school soon. He'd just started when everything fell apart. I said yes, that was perfectly possible, since the government had just announced that the schools were about to reopen. I try to be positive, but I'm not sure he'll be able to follow the lessons. His mind is all over the place, he can't concentrate on even the simplest task. He seems to have forgotten his past, except when sudden flashbacks interrupt his thoughts. The story of what happened to him when he was living in the street changes daily. It's hard for him to distinguish between what's true and what's not, to live in the real world.

I'm not sure I'll be able to look after him properly. However much affection I show him, the smallest thing makes him sad. When he sees my grandchildren with their daddy, he withdraws into a corner and cries. He says it's his fault that his father died. He needs time to forget.

Yes, the epidemic's over. However, Ebola hasn't loosened its grip on us yet. It comforts me to know that there are people who are still thinking of us. Right here, there are some international health organizations that have stayed on, hoping to offer their services to the Ebola survivors who would otherwise never be able to see a doctor. Those are the poorest people, they're the ones who have suffered the most, and they continue to feel the effects of the epidemic. In addition, a number of international NGOs are appealing to the generosity of the global community. They're suggesting to those who have the means that they sponsor these Ebola children and thus create opportunities for their future.

So much remains to be done, all across the board. We have to rebuild our country.

Since the epidemic has been officially over, the decontamination phase of all the treatment centers has now begun. This means that all the high-risk zones where the sick were being treated, and where one cannot enter without a protective suit, will be disinfected until the virus no longer has anywhere to hide. The task is easier in the low-risk zones, which is where the rooms and offices of the medical staff were situated.

Three different categories of equipment have been left behind in the centers, and now is the time to deal with them. Many beds and mattresses can be reused once they've been disinfected, and so can some tables and chairs. But damaged items need to be incinerated, while medical instruments like syringes are disinfected and then buried.

We must remain vigilant. We must build up our strength again and relearn how to live.

XII

In the face of death's absolute power,
poetry offers a little solace.

When she showed the first signs of the disease, there was nothing I could do. I wanted to keep her by my side and care for her. But I knew that would be senseless, I'm not a doctor—if I tended her, she'd have no chance of recovery. If I tended her, we'd both die. I did give it some thought. The two of us, going together.

In her agony, she pleaded with me: "It's Ebola, kill me quick, I'm doomed anyway. I don't want to end my life in horrible suffering. I don't want you to see me like that. Help me." But if there was even the slightest chance she might recover, I had to grasp it.

I called an ambulance to come and pick us up. During the drive, we held hands. When we arrived, we went to the triage tent, which all new patients had to pass through. The medical staff stood two meters away and took our temperatures with an infrared thermometer that was like a pistol pointed at our heads. Then they asked us very specific questions: "Are you vomiting and/or are you bleeding? Are you experiencing nausea? Do you have a sore throat, hiccups, or any other abnormal symptoms? Have you recently been in contact with someone suffering from Ebola?" My fiancée remembered that one of her colleagues at the office had been infected. She also answered yes to several other questions. Since I had just a bit of a fever but no other signs of the illness, I was sent to the area for suspected cases, where I was to wait for my test results to come back from the laboratory. I was distraught when I saw two nurses in protective clothing leading my fiancée to the area reserved for confirmed cases. The sight sent shivers down my spine, and I instantly regretted my decision to bring her to this place. I might never see her again! I was angry with myself for deserting her at the very moment when she had to fight her greatest battle. If she lost, there'd be nothing left of us.

We've been here several days now. Every morning, the nurses take my temperature and assess my health, checking me carefully for any symptoms of infection. My initial test was negative, and now we need to wait for a second one. Suspected cases like me are allowed to walk up and down in the courtyard, read, exercise, and even play cards with the other patients. As for me, I prop a chair against the outside wall of our ward, sheltering from the sun under the corrugated steel roof that casts a thin shadow on the red soil. I sit with my open notebook on my knees, writing poems. Actually, they're not really my own creation. They're poems I know by heart, poems I used to recite to my fiancée, who loved listening to them. I do miss our poetry evenings. When I've finished writing down a poem, I tear the page out of my notebook, fold it in two, and hand it to one of the nurses. I ask them to leave it at the foot of my fiancée's bed. This is my way of being at her side, my way of expressing my great love for her.

> *For a long time now*
> *I've loved to sing your footsteps*
> *And listened to your breath*
> *In the middle of the night*
> *For a long time now your scent*
> *Has invaded all my senses*
> *And your voice sounds in me*
> *A thousand far echoes*
> *For so long, your smile*
> *Has sketched my thoughts*
> *And your nimble fingers*

Have woven my days
So long that I've known
The rhythm of your heartbeat
And the black velvet
*Of your shadow skin**

I had trouble remembering a second one. I see more
and more people arriving at the Ebola center. And I
see more and more people dying. Burial teams appear
and take away the bodies in a hurry. I've become
familiar with this place, with the way it's organized,
and with most of the caregivers. It's a place cut off
from the rest of the world, a place where there's but
little room for hope. I find poetry futile in such a
setting. All I want to do now is spend my time next
to the fence that separates my area from where my
fiancée is. There I can gather some information
about her. I've been told that she remains in critical
condition and that it's still not possible to make any
predictions.

I remember the day we met. At a party at a
friend's house. There was music and plenty of food.
The moment she came into the room, I knew
she'd play an important part in my life. We spent
the evening talking to each other as if nobody else

---

* Extract from *Red Earth / Latérite*, by Véronique Tadjo, translated by Peter S.
Thompson, Eastern Washington University Press, 2006.

existed. And after that, we never parted company. People say we're very much alike, because we have the same mannerisms and laugh at the same jokes. And I'm fairly certain our way of thinking is the same too.

We told our parents we were planning to get married, and started living together. What I love most about her is her gentleness. She's beautiful without being obsessed with her looks. Her eyes are deep, her skin is smooth, her hair is thick. Whenever she smiles at me, I catch myself falling in love with her all over again. The thought of her suffering is intolerable to me. Of her dying? Impossible. She'll soon be discharged, I'm sure of it. Then we can leave this place and resume our life as it was before.

I started writing again. It's the only link left between us, the only way I can express my love to her, the only way I can send her strength. My second poem:

I remember
Diving into your eyes
Discovering each of your features
And listening to your voice
I remember
Sharing with you
A moment in time
Creating a point in space

I remember an everlasting place
Where we baptized
Each minute

She's got to win this war. She must emerge
victorious.

This war, yes, this war. Our country has known
another, just as devastating. A war between men,
between chiefs greedy for power.

Hordes of barefoot fighters, rabid mercenaries,
and soldiers with bloodshot eyes, brandishing
Kalashnikovs, terrorized the city, which was caught
in the middle of a murderous feud. They raped,
pillaged, and massacred people; nothing could stop
them. Child soldiers, recruited for their loyalty
to their warlord and maddened with alcohol and
weed, emptied their firearms on civilians at the
slightest provocation, or even without any apparent
reason. Having spent their childhood in shacks and
in abject poverty, they considered killing no big
deal. The result was wholesale destruction—office
blocks riddled with bullets, schools with caved-
in roofs, ransacked hospitals. People did all they
could to escape the clashes. My parents, my sister,
my two brothers, and I narrowly managed to get
away in our beat-up old car. In the middle of the
night, we found ourselves on roads blocked off
with checkpoints manned by militiamen armed

to the teeth with pistols and machetes. It was like an obstacle course, having to drive along rutted tracks, being forced to make lengthy detours. We were scared, we were hungry, we were thirsty. By the skin of our teeth, more than once, we avoided colliding with troops in armored vehicles. And then, at last, the end of hell: the border post. Five days it took us to get to the other side and be free! We were in exile, just a few kilometers away from our own country. Until the conflict ended, we led wandering, unsettled lives.

As for my fiancée, she told me that when the war was at its peak, her family went into hiding in the bush. Her father had dug a huge hole, a bit like a bunker. That's where they slept at night, after having covered the opening with twigs. When peace was declared at last, we were all overjoyed. We set to work, eager to rebuild our country.

I am scared of death, but not so much for myself. I'm more afraid of losing the one I love. The one who gave me back my will to live.

My second test came back negative, which means that soon I have to leave the center and go back home. I fear this separation. Even if I'm not actually with her, at least I'm not very far. I decide to go back to the barrier and wait. After a while, a male nurse walks toward me. He lowers his gaze and says: "I'm so sorry about your fiancée…"

My last poem isn't a real poem. But it's the only one I've ever written myself. I wanted it to be like a scream, aimed at the sky.

Pain
Throbbing, pulsating
Stinging
It goes right through me

Pain
Freezing, burning
Acrid, bitter
It tears me apart

Pain
Burning, blazing
Oppressing, haunting
Blinding
Deafening

Pain
Lightning flash
To suffer, to die
So cruel

XIII

Knowledge knows no borders;
it has no color and no smell
unknown to Man.

I'm the Congolese researcher who discovered the Ebola virus, right here in my home country. At a time when absolutely nothing was known about the illness, I decided to seek out the place where the first outbreak had occurred in 1976. I harvested several blood samples from a woman stricken with the disease and took them to a laboratory in Belgium to identify this new virus. There it was, under my microscope: long, thin, curled strands of a terrifying elegance.

I strove to analyze it in all its facets in order to find the best way to keep it in check. Scientific experts consider my research "the early phase of an Ebola immunization therapy that's currently being developed."

To this day, I continue my never-ending struggle against the disease at a research institute in Kinshasa. We must provide ourselves with the tools to fight Ebola effectively; we have to block its progress and learn to react quickly if it comes back. A first-generation vaccine against Ebola is already being tested. Others are in the development phase. But further research is definitely required. In collaboration with international health organizations and local governments, a group of scientists has been working on certain experimental serums that seem very promising. However, the pharmaceutical companies want to be sure that there's an actual market, in other words that there's money to be made through the research and development of all these scientific methods. We continually have various epidemics breaking out in one part of the world or another. Which areas of research are the most promising? For financial reasons, certain vaccines that have been developed have never made it to the crucial trial phase. We have the ability to prevent Ebola from resurfacing, but does humanity truly have the will to make this happen?

Be that as it may, other scientists reply, at least we're better prepared for the possibility of another outbreak as we wait for the vaccines. There's better surveillance, the laboratories are showing improved performance, and the population is better informed.

Right now, we have medical teams traveling all over the country, on the lookout for the slightest sign of a recurrence, ready to intervene. Governments have learned to collaborate more efficiently and to share information. Should any new cases of Ebola be diagnosed, they can be brought under control quickly. There will be a handful of deaths, but no more.

That's what we've learned and what we want to retain. However, we cannot ignore the fact that the disease has claimed a large number of health workers, and that as a consequence, there continues to be a lack of them. We should train more, and we should take special care of them. How else can they really do their job? They need to be taught to detect cases of infection extremely rapidly, to screen them and to deal with them without putting themselves in danger. Without their involvement, the system is bound to collapse.

And now the zoologists have joined in. They claim to have discovered a phenomenon that greatly increases Ebola's catastrophic impact. When an outbreak is about to happen in a forest region, the virus will leave gruesome traces in the natural environment. It attacks antelopes, deer, and rodents, but especially big apes such as chimpanzees, which it strikes with devastating effect. The remains of hundreds of animals are scattered on the ground

among the trees, right where they collapsed,
overcome by the illness. Whenever the villagers
notice an unusual number of wild animal carcasses,
they've learned to alert the local authorities at once,
since the carcasses signify that an Ebola outbreak
among humans is about to happen.

People call me a scholar, a man for whom science
equals truth and nothing but the truth. But I've
understood one thing: scientific reason can't satisfy
every human need. In the fight against Ebola, human
beings have always been more important than
everything else. They are the agents of their own
recovery, their own safety.

And in this race against the clock, the ancestors
too are making their voices heard. They are the true
protectors, the great allies of the living. The hospital
is a failure. An ugly, anonymous death sentence,
devoid of compassion, without a soul. A place where
the poor end their lives miserably, inside dilapidated
buildings.

In the villages and in certain parts of the city,
the traditional healer is still in possession of some
ancestral knowledge. His calming words and solemn
gestures come from a past resolved to hold its ground.
He's a formidable rival. Those who look upon his
authority with disdain have allowed themselves to be
deluded. For people versed in traditional medicine,
there's more at stake than just plants and vegetation.

It's an expression of a complete worldview, a way of living in synergy with fauna and flora. To those who come to him for a consultation, the traditional healer will say one of the following four sentences:

It's a disease I know and am able to heal.

It's a disease I know but can't heal.

It's a disease I don't know, but I can heal it.

It's a disease I don't know and can't heal.

Right there and then, everything can change. History may be rewritten, and mentalities may evolve. Cooperation can begin. At the outset in the fight against Ebola, no one paid any attention to the traditional healers. Government bodies ignored them just as much as the NGOs and the health professionals. Considered ignorant and incompetent at dealing with the illness, they were accused of only making things worse. But despite all the efforts the scientists were making, the illness continued its rampage. What could be done? The specialists knew they had to rethink their strategy and get much closer to the people. Traditional healers share the population's daily lives, their environment, their interests. They're prepared to cover great distances on foot to visit a patient, and when they arrive, they're not content just to treat the body; they care for the whole person.

So yes, we had to make an appeal to them!

Their medicine is something familiar to the majority of the population.

It's readily accessible.

It doesn't cost much.

It forms part of our culture.

It inspires confidence and reassures people.

It has, in other words, all the qualities that Western medicine in Africa has either lost or never managed to acquire.

The traditional healers were told all the relevant facts about Ebola, so they could pass on these explanations to their patients, thus helping to educate them. And that's how they ended up persuading their patients to go and be treated by those "who know about the disease."

Please understand that as a scientist, I want to seek out what's effective in every realm of knowledge. We have only one life, and it takes place on earth. No other option is available to us. Through our thoughts, our words, and our actions, we have the capacity to reconstruct the world. This is my conviction, my religion, my raison d'être. I believe in the existence of pure energy.

Every single human being is a universe.

Man is made up of water, oxygen, carbon, hydrogen, nitrogen, calcium, phosphorus, potassium, sulfur, sodium, chlorine, iron, magnesium, zinc, manganese, copper, iodine, cobalt, nickel, aluminum, lead, tin, titanium, fluoride, bromine, arsenic, and more.

The atoms making up our body come from deep inside the stars.

Yes, really, from deep inside the stars!

Almost all the atoms of the universe are formed in the center of these celestial bodies. Furnace. Fusion. Astronomers say that stars shine for billions of years, their bubbling bellies giving birth to billions of atoms. Then, one day, the star dies. The atoms composing it expand in space, turning into metals, minerals, water, and living beings.

In order to reconstitute itself, our organism has to produce organic matter on a daily basis. But the human body does not know how to do this. Only plants have the ability to make oxygen and compose organic molecules from inorganic matter. Animals are equally unable to produce organic matter. So they eat plants, or, if they are carnivores, they devour animals that feed on plants. We are the same. We cannot survive without plants. We eat animals.

The stars, the oceans, plants, and animals are the building blocks of our bodies.

The universe doesn't exist outside of us. It's in us.

We are the universe.

But of all this immeasurable beauty, this unfathomable mystery, what do we have left?

Deep
Inside the
Forest

XIV

*The chilling voice of Ebola rings out
in the early morning.*

All right, all well and good, but it's not me humans ought to fear the most. They should rather be scared of themselves!

I'm a virus thousands of years old. I belong to the large family of the Filoviridae. People have known about me for only forty years or so. Nevertheless, I've been around for a very long time in this extraordinary forest, referred to as "primeval," where everything has remained pristine since the beginning of time.

I have five brothers: Ebola Zaire, the most virulent among us; Ebola Sudan, which follows hard on its heels; Ebola Ivory Coast, so discreet that humans became acquainted with it only in 1994, thanks to a single patient, who incidentally didn't die, but recovered; Ebola Bundibugyo, which lives in Uganda; and, finally, Ebola Reston, which has settled in Asia, where it has yet to show its full potential.

I don't like to travel. I prefer to stay put right here, deep in the primordial jungle, which is where I'm happiest. Except when someone comes and disturbs me. Except when someone comes and disturbs my host. Because when I'm abruptly awakened from my sleep, I move from one animal to the next. I often choose great apes—gorillas or chimpanzees—but also the antelopes humans are so fond of. The animals in the jungle all know each other. They have their habitual meeting places, for example around watering holes, or under fruit trees colonized by bats. It's no secret what happens next. A man violates nature by pulling the trigger and killing an animal. He cuts up the carcass. Blood on his hands. Fresh blood on his hands. Red blood on his hands. He lays the animal across his shoulders and takes it to the village. He doesn't know that I've already entered his body. Or that very shortly I'll be in his family. In his entire community. I move quietly and slowly in the beginning, but soon comes the grand finale, the fire, the flames.

It's not me that has changed. It's humankind, which has changed direction. The lives men lead today are no longer the lives the Old Ones led.

They've become more demanding, greedier, more
predatory. Their appetites are limitless.

I know nothing about their beliefs. I'm not
governed by any law. I'm here purely for the sake of
existing. I am me, period. An organism that needs
to reproduce itself. No compromise. No negotiation.
I'm alive, and I'm prepared to do whatever it takes
to stay that way. My only needs are to feed and to
defend myself. A pile of flesh will do. Any kind of
receptacle, animal or human, it's all the same to me.
I'm neither good nor bad. Such judgments are useless.
I'm like a plant that grows, like a spider that devours
its prey.

What humans don't seem to understand is that I
have no predilection for them. They die too fast, too
awfully. They're not useful to my goals. If our paths
happen to cross, why not, but if they don't, I won't
seek them out. It's they who come to me.

We, the viruses, have succeeded in conquering
the planet. We're in the sea, we're in the air. We're
everywhere. We reinvent ourselves by mutating and
multiplying with increasing speed. Man can't figure
us out. The antibiotics he's so proud of have absolutely
no effect on us. We can cross borders and continents at
will. To our credit, we kill germs and bacteria by the
thousands. And yet no one would dream of thanking
us for our assistance, so what's the point?

Given the choice, I would clip humanity's
wings to prevent them from flying. Then they'd
have to crawl in the dust, and they'd get a better
understanding of life. No one can defeat me. No one
can wipe me out. If I withdraw, it's just a strategic
retreat. As soon as a new opportunity presents itself,
I'll be back. The greatest scientists on earth have
tried, but so far, they still haven't managed to crack
my genetic code. I'm an equation they can't solve.
When I enter a body, I go through the blood vessels
in order to invade the vital organs: liver, spleen,
pancreas, lungs, kidneys, thyroid gland, skin, brain.
A few days is all I need to overcome the pathetic little
obstacles I encounter along the way!

Humans lament their fate, but they're no better
than I am. They have no lessons to teach to anyone.
They should instead take a hard look at the evil they
have inflicted and continue to inflict on themselves,
deliberately, ever since they first walked the earth.

They are destructive by nature, much more so
than I am. And yet, although they are perfectly aware
of that fact, they refuse to acknowledge it. They
prefer to delude themselves, to believe themselves
superior to the other creatures in this world. Rulers,
tyrants of this planet, that's what they are, and their
power is absolute. Their arrogance has made them
forget every limit. Worse, they slaughter one another
without mercy, and they come up with crueler ways

of tormenting and killing every single day. They
always find new reasons for starting wars.

Do you know what my favorite song is, Baobab?
It's Zao's "Ancien combattant"—"War Veteran."
Better than any lecture, it illustrates what's so
grotesque about Man and his incurable, pathological
destructiveness. The musician uses the absurd to
show that he's understood everything. I can recite the
words for you—I know them well:

> *Cadence count, one, two*
> *War veteran Mundasukiri*
> *Cadence count, one, two*
> *War veteran Mundasukiri*
>
> *The world wars*
> *Aren't pretty, they're not nice*
> *The world wars*
> *Aren't pretty, they're not nice*
> *When the world war comes*
> *Everyone's cadavered*
> *When the world war comes*
> *Everyone's cadavered*
> *When the bullet's whistling, no*
> *time left to choose*
> *If you don't dance the changui*
> *fast, my dear, oh! you're*
> *Cadavered*

Whacked with a club
All of a sudden, wham, cadavered

Your wife cadavered
Your mother cadavered
Your grandfather cadavered
Your kids cadavered
The kings cadavered
The queens cadavered
The emperors cadavered
All the presidents cadavered
The ministers cadavered
The bodyguards cadavered
The bikers cadavered
The soldiers cadavered
The civilians cadavered
The cops cadavered
The gendarmes cadavered
The workers cadavered
The jobless cadavered
Your sweetheart cadavered
Your first mistress cadavered
Your second mistress cadavered
Beer cadavered
Whiskey cadavered
Red wine cadavered
Palm wine cadavered
Music lovers cadavered

Everybody cadavered
Me myself cadavered

Cadence count, a-one, a-two
War veteran Mundasukiri
Cadence count, a-one, a-two
*War veteran Mundasukiri**

It's time for people to realize something: they aren't
good, they've never been good. Never, at any
time! Let them get that straight, once and for all.
They're imperfect and incomplete. They're mortal.
Everything rots. Everything disintegrates. Everything
merges with the ground. Sometimes, their God
sprinkles a handful of hopes onto the world and then
goes back to His bed in the glowing darkness. The
reddish wound of the firmament, the tumultuous
waters, the scorching wind, the devouring floods—
their God watches all that from afar. He makes them
suffer within Him. Without Him.

You don't believe me, Baobab? You shake the
crest of your foliage?

You surely know that horror follows barbarism
with them. Even when they declare themselves to
be righters of wrongs, warriors in a good cause,

---

* Zao (Congolese author, singer, and composer), "Ancien combattant," 1984.

they still have dirty hands. The truth is they're not fighting for an ideal. They don't kill in the service of the common good, no; they kill because the inhumanity of one group quite simply justifies the savagery of another. Whether they engage in mutual massacre with clubs, knives, spears, arrows and hatchets, like our ancestors, or use machine guns, grenades, shells, bombs, and chemical weapons, it comes down to the same things: atrocities, massacres, genocides. Where and when is it all going to stop? How much longer do we have to wait until humanity comes to its senses?

Do you want me to shut up, Baobab?

No, I haven't finished. I have to add that human self-hatred is a generalized thing, to which racial or gender differences are as irrelevant as differences of religion or belief, of education or socioeconomic status. None of this matters; one of these days, they'll start their mutual killings again. They themselves cannot perceive that the barbarism they abhor lives in their own souls and sows terror in all four corners of the world. It takes them by surprise every single time.

I can see your leaves quivering, Baobab, your trunk's losing its sheen. I beg you, don't take refuge in denial!

I don't try to figure out who's right or wrong in humankind's innumerable wars; I simply observe the extent of their capacity for self-destruction.

I could go on, but I prefer to stop now, I've said enough.

Believe me, Baobab, if Man could only acknowledge his dark side as an intrinsic part of his being, he'd surely get better at keeping his destructive instincts under control, instead of letting himself be controlled by them. Humans should just step back, examine themselves dispassionately, and look for effective ways of ending the carnage. They should forget their absurd ideas about brotherhood and solidarity, which they shamelessly flout anyway, and become more realistic.

It distresses me to see how intent the human race is on its own destruction. Very soon, there will be nothing left for me to do. Human beings should be given as little power as possible. No kings, no princes, no heads of state, no politicians, just mere individuals facing their destiny. Because all forms of government, which are supposed to establish order, actually create chaos. They're veritable mafias, run by the rich, who monopolize assets and resources.

To tell the truth, I fear only one thing: seeing human beings go against their nefarious nature and start to help each other. For it was neither science nor money that made me retreat when I was already so close to my goal. No, it was ordinary people, who gradually came to understand that their impact would be greater if they put their immediate interests and personal troubles aside in order to think, work, and fight collectively. They surprised me. That was the moment when I was obliged to withdraw and accept my defeat. I understood that their true power showed itself when they presented a united front.

Maybe humans are afraid of me because I remind them how fragile and evanescent life is. From one day to the next, everything can change. Chance is inscribed in their genes. They're born by chance, by the accidental nature of existence.

And besides, they should know that I'm not the only one capable of annihilating them.

A natural disaster could destroy the earth much faster than I can. The earth could collide with another planet, be swallowed by a black hole, or bombarded by meteorites.

There is, of course, the threat of a nuclear war between "civilized" countries, a conflict of such magnitude that it could wipe out all life. Assuming that extraterrestrials haven't wiped out the earthlings by then. If they manage to escape from all of that, the sun isn't going to leave them unscathed. Because the sun itself is doomed to die. But before it goes out, it will shine more brightly than ever before. The intolerable heat this brings will dry up most of the water. The earth's blood will spill into the atmosphere, and the globe will be emptied and become a shriveled fruit with no juice, an empty shell.

Then the regal celestial body will turn into
a freezing, indifferent mass, and that mass will
gradually dissolve into space. And the universe will
forget that there was ever a time when a sun seething
with energy had reigned supreme.

XV

The voice of the Bat joins in to counter Ebola's voice.

There's no obligation that ties me to Ebola, other than the duty of protecting and preserving Nature. But first of all, let's set the record straight: I'm not to blame for this tragedy. It has happened entirely against my will. I wish no one harm.

As a bat, somewhere midway between a mammal and a bird, with my foxy-looking fangs and snout and my translucent wings, I harbor but one regret: having let Ebola escape from my belly. It was dormant in me until Man came and wrecked the splendor of the forest. I had offered the virus the warmth of my blood and the whole multitude of my species. We're timid but hospitable creatures, we feed on ripe fruit or insects, we're peaceful, and we sleep a lot, hanging upside down in trees, clinging to the branches with our feet.

I usually prefer to stay with the group, huddling up against the soft, warm, furry skin of the others, breathing in the odor of the colony. When we take flight at nightfall, our screeching and squeaking can be heard far and wide.

As a bat, somewhere midway between a mammal and a bird, with my foxy-looking fangs and snout and my translucent wings, I harbor but one regret: having let Ebola escape from my belly. Before it started targeting Man, it was attacking the monkeys, the friends of the forest, as if testing its own power. I know them well, since we're neighbors and sometimes even share the same trees. I've seen their numbers shrink at a staggering speed, although all they really want is to live among their own kind. When it's not Ebola that decimates them, it's humans, who hunt them for their meat or to sell them to laboratories, circuses, or zoos. I've seen monkeys get themselves killed while trying to protect one of their troop. The females sacrifice themselves for the sake of saving their young. They rear them for several years and grow very attached to them. At night, monkeys go to sleep high up in a tree. Like us, they love fruit, but they also feed on tender leaves or juicy blossoms, and, from time to time, they devour a small animal. They have a language that consists of screeching and grimacing. They spread seeds in the ground, just as farmers do, keeping the forest alive.

I fear for them, because they've lost a great deal.
They're surrounded on every side.

Is it my fault if Ebola has left my belly and is now
spreading panic among humans and animals? What
was I supposed to do about that? I thought we had an
agreement it was content with.

But look at me now, I'm the one that gets
demonized.

No, I do not suck human blood! No, I am not
evil! No, I'm not a wandering spirit! And no, I'm not
a symbol of death and disease!

I'm a creature that augurs good luck, I form part
of Nature just like the others.

For I was born from love.

One of the greatest griots of our time knows the
story of my origin. Here it is.

I was born in the dead of night, in a beautiful
forest, high up in the crown of a kind and
welcoming tree. My mother came from the
family of the birds, a dove with gray-brown
feathers with a finely chiseled beak. She was
famous for her beauty and her melodious
cooing.

One day, a wild fox was roaming around
the area, eager for fresh meat. He would
devour palm rats, hares, does, and even birds
if they made the mistake of swooping so

low that he could catch them. This is what happened with my mother: one day she was busy pulling a worm out of the ground when she suddenly found herself face-to-face with the fox. He was about to crunch her bones in his wide-open muzzle when their eyes met, and it was love at first sight. The fox was entranced by the dove's plumage, which shone in the crystalline light as it fell across the foliage of the trees and came to rest on the two animals. As for my mother, the fox's thick, ocher-colored fur and piercing gaze, in which she saw severity but also great sadness, plunged her into a strange confusion.

That was the beginning of an improbable love that cared nothing for their differences or for the ensuing scandal, which would surely agitate the animal community. My mother told me that they found refuge amid the roots of a tree sympathetic to their plight. My father was so smitten that he stopped hunting. After having long since given up all hope of knowing happiness, he had found it at last.

At the time of my birth, my mother withdrew to the top of their tree in order to bring me into the world. That's how I came to be born, I, the bat, half mammal, half bird, with the claws and muzzle of a fox and translucent wings.*

Yes, I'm a hybrid and proud of it. We're all hybrids, human-like animals, or animal-like humans. All of us have a bright side as well as a dark side. Our lives are not so much a straight line as a squiggle that meanders or goes round and round in circles and sometimes finally finds its direction. Millions of life forms have appeared and disappeared throughout the ages. We have to be versatile and able to adapt, not hard like a rock, dried-up in mind and body. We need to know how to deal with the unexpected. The universe—with the innumerable planets of the cosmos, the diversity of earthly creatures, and the infinity of possible destinies—proves it every day.

Humans, alas, are still dreaming of a purity that doesn't exist, of a unity that has never been achieved. That's why some of them can't stop searching for a higher power through science. "In reality," Man says, "we create more than we destroy. We save more lives than we kill. We discover medicines that cure and vaccines that protect. Our advanced technologies will provide solutions for our problems and innovations will alleviate global hunger and warfare. Today,

---

* Inspired by the writer and ethnologist Amadou Hampâté Bâ's tale on the origin of the bat.

we're all interlinked via fiber-optic networks that cover the planet in every direction. And Nature will even benefit from our discoveries. Having to use muscle power to accomplish a task is a thing of the past—machines will do it for us. Gone are the days when we had to exhaust our natural resources—other energy sources will become available. Ways and means will be found to clean up our polluted water, to purify the air we breathe, to stop the glaciers from melting and the oceans from rising. We can do it." That's the way men think. I'd love to believe them. Their words can embellish everything. They know how to dream and to create, driven by nothing but their desire to achieve perfection.

But I know none of this will actually happen unless they learn to share with one another, with us, and with every creature yet to be born.

Human beings will never be "demigods." Like trees, they have roots that run deep. Like mammals, they're warm-blooded. Their body determines their longevity, but in the end, it disappears and liberates them from the trials and tribulations of life.

Humans need to recognize that they're part of the world, that there's a close bond between them and all other living creatures, great and small. Instead of trying to rise above their earthly origins. Instead of wanting to conceal the presence of death by dint of ever-more-sophisticated inventions.

Instead of turning a blind eye to the sufferings of life, they should learn to prepare for them and to accept the pure joy of being in the world.

Conscious, once and for all, of the danger they pose to their own species as well as to the entire biosphere, they should make use of their great intelligence to prevent the end of the world.

Colonizing space with enormous rockets will almost certainly not be a lifeline for them. For if they haven't learned to live here, how can they possibly survive in the distant Beyond?

The
Epidemic
Is
Contained

XVI

The Whispering Tree

I, Baobab, am the first tree, the everlasting tree, the totem tree. My crown touches the heavens and offers the world below refreshing shade. I yearn toward soft, life-sustaining light, that it may brighten humanity, illuminate darkness, and soothe fear.

I have heard Ebola's voice; I shall not respond to its maliciousness. It has no comprehension of Man—in its desire to absolve itself, it considers only Man's faults.

I have heard Bat's voice; I agree with her. I would add that the human race ought to sign a covenant of mutual understanding with Nature. We need to live together and preserve the well-being of our planet.

Everything has been said. Everything remains to be said.

But, for the moment, let's forget all this, the hour of celebration has come. The relief in everyone's heart is like honey dripping into the mouth of a hunter who's been lost in the forest.

Ebola's gone! Ebola's gone!

The epidemic is officially over. The president of the country has solemnly announced it. The public health authorities have repeated it. The World Health Organization has confirmed it. In order to celebrate this joyful news, a piece of music is broadcast on the airwaves of the national radio over and over: "Bye Bye Ebola." The miracle of finally being free: *"Nobody wanna see you risin'...I tank God dat it's gone...Now watch me do Azonto!"*

I'm told that the song has gone around the world. The video shows the president in his spacious office, making the V sign for victory. There are doctors dressed like astronauts, nurses in their blue garb, soldiers in fatigues, schoolchildren in their uniforms, and vendors making dance moves in front of their stalls, swirling, jumping in the air, clapping their hands, and doing Azonto dance steps. From time to time they stop, laughing and shaking each other by the hand—such an ordinary gesture, but forbidden when the epidemic was raging. They'll be able to kiss one another again. They'll be able to embrace and touch one another again.

It's over! It's over!

In the center of the capital city, thousands of people come together to celebrate the end of the epidemic. Scenes of immense happiness. Jubilation. Lit candles. Fireworks. The crowd spills out into the streets, dancing and shouting for joy. Singing and weeping, they vent their emotions.

In the bars, beer is flowing freely and the music's deafening. Women sway to the rhythms of languorous tunes, their silhouettes shimmering under the artificial lights. They're wearing tight dresses and high heels. The patrons have come to toast the defeat of Ebola. There's something desperate in their desire to forget and to have fun at all costs. They foresee the return of investors to the country, an end to the economic decline, and the start of large-scale public works projects. They think they've demonstrated courage and shown their determination to overcome the most colossal hardships. They raise their glasses and sigh with relief, it's OK to breathe again, and it will finally be possible to think of something else. Death has brushed past us, but we have survived!

Bye-bye, Ebola!

Life has started up again, even in the most far-flung corners of the country. In my village, the men are coming once more to sit in the shade of my foliage. Under my protective gaze, they rest on their multicolored mats, having shared a meal that had been jointly prepared by each family. Digging into large platters with their hands, they had savored rice balls and a few chunks of meat.

Small children are clinging to their mothers,
sucking their breasts. Curious young goats are
coming close to watch things getting back to normal.
I prick up my ears, listening to what the villagers
have to say. An old woman with soft, shoulder-length
gray braids stands up. She looks concerned, but she
nevertheless addresses the rest of the group with a
smile on her face: "We may have regained our peace,
but let's remain vigilant. After dying several times
over, we must learn again how to live."

I suddenly feel affection for these survivors,
whom I recognize, and I weep with them for those
that have died.

At nightfall, the balafons and koras come out.
Poets begin to chant the courageous exploits of the
heroes in the struggle.

Tomorrow, the men will return to their activities:
the deserted fields awaiting their attention; the herds
of cattle bellowing in their enclosures; the barns
ready to shelter grain for the coming seasons.

And I'm left alone for the night. I can see the
moon's delicate outlines etched into the star-speckled
vault of the sky above. I listen to the trees that grow
over there in the forest. It will be reborn from those
young seedlings.

The wheel of fortune and disaster never ceases
to turn. Joy already bears within itself the sadness
of attrition. Strength to achieve a renewal may arise

from a disaster. Everything happens deep down, everything happens underneath the earth's surface. I will pass on to the shrubs my roots' sap.

And the destiny of Man will become one with ours.

On March 21, 2014, an Ebola outbreak was declared in Guinea.

On March 31, 2014, an Ebola outbreak was declared in Liberia.

On May 26, 2014, an Ebola outbreak was declared in Sierra Leone.

In March 2016, the outbreak officially ended in Guinea and Sierra Leone, and in June 2016 in Liberia.

Final toll: 28,646 people were infected, and 11,323 people died (these numbers probably don't take victims of related diseases into account).

ACKNOWLEDGMENTS

My gratitude goes to the many scientists, medical personnel, survivors, journalists, academic researchers, international institutions, and donors who contributed to public knowledge and my knowledge of the Ebola epidemic. I have drawn parallels between the three affected countries in terms of the suffering that befell them, but more than anything else, I was inspired by the courage of all those involved in the fight against the virus. A vaccine for the prevention of the Ebola virus disease has been found to be safe and effective against the *Zaire ebolavirus* species only. Several investigational vaccines are now being tested. The response to the Covid-19 pandemic in West Africa has been strengthened by the lessons learned during the Ebola epidemic.

I would like to thank Judith Gurewich, my publisher, for her guidance, John Cullen for his work on this translation, and Alexandra Poreda, Yvonne Cárdenas, and John Rambow for their careful editing.

To Nick, Larry, and Matteo, *merci* for your unwavering support.

VÉRONIQUE TADJO is a writer, poet, novelist, and artist from Côte d'Ivoire. She earned a doctorate in Black American Literature and Civilization from the Sorbonne, Paris IV, and went to the United States as a Fulbright scholar at Howard University in Washington, DC. She headed the French Department of the University of the Witwatersrand in Johannesburg until 2015. Her books have been translated into several languages, from *The Blind Kingdom* (1991) to *The Shadow of Imana: Travels in the Heart of Rwanda* (2001) and *Queen Pokou: Concerto for a Sacrifice* (2005), which was awarded the Grand Prix de Littérature d'Afrique Noire in 2005.